Samuel French Acting Edition

How to Survive an Apocalypse

by Jordan Hall

I0591883

‖SAMUEL FRENCH‖

SAMUELFRENCH.COM   SAMUELFRENCH.CO.UK

FOR PRODUCTION ENQUIRIES

UNITED STATES AND CANADA
Info@SamuelFrench.com
1-866-598-8449

UNITED KINGDOM AND EUROPE
Plays@SamuelFrench.co.uk
020-7255-4302

Each title is subject to availability from Samuel French, depending upon country of performance. Please be aware that *HOW TO SURVIVE AN APOCALYPSE* may not be licensed by Samuel French in your territory. Professional and amateur producers should contact the nearest Samuel French office or licensing partner to verify availability.

MUSIC USE NOTE

Licensees are solely responsible for obtaining formal written permission from copyright owners to use copyrighted music in the performance of this play and are strongly cautioned to do so. If no such permission is obtained by the licensee, then the licensee must use only original music that the licensee owns and controls. Licensees are solely responsible and liable for all music clearances and shall indemnify the copyright owners of the play(s) and their licensing agent, Samuel French, against any costs, expenses, losses and liabilities arising from the use of music by licensees. Please contact the appropriate music licensing authority in your territory for the rights to any incidental music.

IMPORTANT BILLING AND CREDIT REQUIREMENTS

If you have obtained performance rights to this title, please refer to your licensing agreement for important billing and credit requirements.

HOW TO SURVIVE AN APOCALYPSE was initially created during an artistic residency at Pi Theatre with support from the British Columbia Arts Council. Subsequent to this, the play was developed through Flying Start, a partnership of Touchstone Theatre and the Playwrights Theatre Centre giving a stage to new professional playwrights.

HOW TO SURVIVE AN APOCALYPSE premiered at the Firehall Arts Centre on June 2, 2016 in Vancouver, British Columbia. It was premiered by Touchstone Theatre in association with the Playwrights Theatre Centre and the Firehall Arts Centre. The director was Katrina Dunn, with sets by David Roberts, costumes by Christopher David Gauthier, lighting by Adrian Muir, and sound by Elliot Vaughan. The dramaturg was Kathleen Flaherty and the stage manager was Rebecca Mulvihill. The cast was as follows:

JEN . . . . Claire Hesselgrave

TIM . . . . Sebastien Archibald

ABBY. . . . . Lindsey Angell

BRUCE . . . . .Zahf Paroo

Awards and Distinctions:
2014 PGC Tom Hendry Award – Comedy *(Shortlisted)*
2015 La Mama Umbria International Playwrights Retreat *(Official Selection)*
2016 Flying Start Award – Playwrights Theatre Centre, Touchstone Theatre, Firehall Arts Centre *(First Prize)*

CHARACTERS

JEN – late-twenties/early thirties-ish, a little bit hip, successful enough

TIM – the same, maybe not quite as hip

ABBY – almost thirty, hoping for enlightenment

BRUCE – early thirties, slick-as-hell

AUTHOR'S NOTES

An **Apocalypse** (Ancient Greek: ἀποκάλυψις, from ἀπό and καλύπτω meaning "uncovering"), translated literally from Greek, is a disclosure of knowledge, i.e. a lifting of the veil or revelation.

I think it was 2013 when I started thinking seriously about the Apocalypse. As a fan of mythology and science fiction, I've always loved its various incarnations: Wars of the gods, zombies, meteors, plagues, environmental disaster. Give me a struggling dystopia or a post-apocalyptic wasteland and I'm hooked.

But in 2013 – as we limped back from the 2008 financial crisis; as Edward Snowden disclosed a massive government surveillance program; as one of the warmest years on record concluded with the devastation of Typhoon Haiyan – the end of the world took on a different character. Why was I so fascinated by fictional devastation when there was so much real disaster to go around? I realized that what I loved about the Apocalypse wasn't the event itself, but the stories of what came after – I found disaster compelling because I thought I was going to survive it.

I wasn't alone. All over North America, there were people who felt the exact same way: Preppers. On the surface, Prepping made perfect sense. We were destroying our environment; corporations and the one percent were grinding the bones of the impoverished to make their bread – human civilization was clearly doomed. Why not stockpile canned goods and a couple of rifles in the hopes you could outlast everyone else's stupidity?

Except...the more I researched, the more Prepping seemed like another fantasy. The idea that any amount of preparation could protect me from such vast forces? It was like believing perfect grades could save you from failure; or that a perfect life could save you from death. And suddenly there was Jen, and there was Tim, and of course the best way to grapple with my anxiety about the Apocalypse was to write a play about it.

At its heart, *How to Survive an Apocalypse* is a comedy of remarriage – a sub-genre of the romantic comedy that I came to love through plays like *Private Lives* and films like *The Philadelphia Story*. It's a genre in which the mistakes and misconceptions of the past have to be cleared away before we can begin again, and so it is for Jen and Tim and many young adults these days. The old milestones of success and adulthood may well be unattainable for us. If we're going to build lasting relationships and lives, we have to figure out what old ideas to clear away, and where to begin again.

So here's to our Apocalypse. May we all find a way to survive it.

Some Brief Thoughts on Retrofitting and Set Design

Retrofitting

I tend to write plays for a specific time and place, and *How to Survive an Apocalypse* is very much a portrait of young adults in the post-financial crash reality of Vancouver, British Columbia. That said, I suspect that much of what is resonant for Vancouver may well be resonant for other large urban centres – and that references to specific locations in the play can usually be adjusted to fit a new city very easily. In general, I've found that audiences respond to the immediacy of a play set in their environs more personally than to one that seems geographically removed. If, as a producer, such a retrofitting of the text interests you, please reach out to your Samuel French licensing representative.

Set Design

As a piece that tackles materialism, and which uses the sheer accumulation of "stuff" to provide both a sense of the overwhelming ethos of the times and as a metaphor for the difficulties and claustrophobia of a relationship, *How to Survive an Apocalypse* is a prop-heavy show. It is essential to a successful staging to let the gradual influx, first of survival supplies and then of wires and other simulation accessories, move the aesthetic of the apartment set from streamlined to cluttered and chaotic over the course of the show. In particular, I would recommend a staging where Tim and Jen's apartment is central, and serves as a locus for this accumulation, and where other locales – Jen's office, restaurants, and even the camping scenes – are outgrowths of the apartment set. Not only does this allow the growing chaos of the apartment to inflect the scenes in other locales, but allowing props to move into the set and then remain there prevents long and time-consuming set changes. On a personal note, most of the clutter described is made up of common household items and emergency supplies – if you must purchase it instead of sourcing it from within the production and company, please do your best to have it absorbed by the company after the show, in an effort to reduce the production's footprint.

ACKNOWLEDGEMENTS

Kathleen Flaherty & PTC
Katrina Dunn & Touchstone
Donna Spencer & The Firehall Arts Centre
Richard Wolfe & Pi Theatre
Kendra Fanconi & The Only Animal
BCAC
Eatwild & Singing Lands
Delvin Solkinson & Gaiacraft Vancouver
Daniel Zomparelli
James Daniell

A Special Note

If you are a Housing Equity Organization or similar type of charity considering staging an amateur production of *How to Survive an Apocalypse* as a fundraiser, please contact your licensing representative at Samuel French, as the playwright has made provisions for the donation of her portion of the play's royalties back to your organization, provided your group and the proposed production meet certain criteria.

For Dave, with whom I would share a 300-square-foot fallout shelter.
And for Charlie, in the hope that none of us have to.

"So I think the world will come to an end amid the general applause from all the wits who believe that it is a joke."
– Søren Kierkegaard

ACT ONE

Scene One

(A hipster-chic loft. Maybe trying a little too hard. **JEN GREEN***, less pretty than cool, applies eyeliner while her husband,* **TIM GREEN***, weedy and goateed, lies propped up on the couch, clicking away at a laptop.)*

JEN. ...So she's up there, in front of the whole board – having already hired this consultant, mind you – going on about how we have to focus on our "target identity." As though the issue is even a marketing issue and not a by-product of the collapse of Western Civilization –

TIM. ...Uh-huh.

JEN. And she explains that our target identity – this imbecilic "person who the magazine should be"? Should be a hipster. But not some retro-loser hipster – the implication being *me* or really anybody without a trust fund. Not that hipster, no.

TIM. ...Uh-huh.

JEN. Our magazine is the kind of hipster who collects seven hundred dollar sneakers and has an all-white penthouse in Gastown. So – a douchebag. The whole publishing industry is in a decade-long death-spiral, and Elspeth thinks the solution is to rebrand my magazine as some guy she did at a house party one time. But it's fine, because she gets to spend money we don't have hiring this corporate snake oil salesman to "save us." Like, shit. Face facts. Don't just put on a tin-foil hat and call it a silver lining.

TIM. ...Uh-huh.

JEN. Sweetie. Pay less attention. Your apathy's hot.

TIM. Sorry. I'm just trying to tweak these splatter physics. Something's off in the blood dynamics.

JEN. The trials and tribulations of working with zombies.

> *(Beat.)*

How much longer is that going to take? We should have left five minutes ago.

TIM. I have to finish this, Jen. My portfolio is like ninety percent of getting the job. A former gig coding world engines for indies doesn't make me a shoe-in for a zombie slasher franchise.

JEN. Who are these guys again?

TIM. They're the ones making Torso IV. Or maybe V. There have been a lot of Torsos.

JEN. God. I can't believe you're even putting in a portfolio.

TIM. Yeah, well, after six months on the dole, I'm putting in a portfolio for everything. You can't keep me in Pabst and hummus chips forever.

JEN. You mean I won't be coming home to a grown man who's been sitting around in his boxers all day?

> *(Off* **TIM***'s look:)*

No. I don't mean that. What I mean is it's shitty Ergodic Arts went under. You're a genius. You shouldn't have to chase jobs coding for some brainless gore fest.

TIM. Yeah. Well. In surprising news, life's not fair.

JEN. Don't I know it. If we don't get to this thing and start running damage control, Elspeth'll have this guy lobotomizing my magazine before they've finished the appies.

> *(She darts into another room and returns with a pair of slacks.)*

Pants.

> *(***TIM*** dutifully puts on the pants, but promptly goes back to working on the laptop.)*

TIM. Oh c'mon, Elspeth couldn't get the rest of the board to change a font size without you.

JEN. That was back when I was the hot new thing, with ambitious plans and a surplus to match. Our operating deficit is making the board twitchy.

> *(She notices something amiss with her eyeliner and pulls out a compact to correct it.)*

It's making me twitchy.

TIM. You're still the coolest girl in the room.

> *(He puts aside his laptop and pulls her down onto the couch. She doesn't stop fixing her eyeliner.)*

Editor of Vancouver's answer to the *New Yorker* –

JEN. With a board chair who's gunning for my job –

TIM. With her cushy pad –

JEN. A rental *we* can barely afford anymore –

TIM. And her devilishly handsome husband...

> *(He starts kissing her neck.)*

JEN. Stop that! It took me like half-an-hour to get this eyeliner right.

TIM. You don't need it.

JEN. You're sweet. But yes I do.

> *(She puts away the compact and heads to the closet to pick out a dress shirt and a jacket.)*

We pretend to be all progressive but no one listens to ugly feminists. If you aren't better looking than fifty percent of the room, they write you off as biased.

TIM. All you have to do is start talking and it's Shock and Awe, and you know it.

JEN. Which is *exactly* why I need you to put on a decent jacket and be the adoring husband. On my own I'm that bitch who won't stop talking. With you on my arm I'm abrasive, but charming.

TIM. I am a versatile accessory.

JEN. As status symbols go, husbands are right up there.

> *(She pecks him on the cheek.)*

Now get a move on.

> *(She's draping the shirt and jacket over his shoulders, but he shoos her hands away and puts the jacket on over his t-shirt. This done, he opens up the laptop again.)*

TIM. You know if I land this job, it'll take some of the pressure off you.

JEN. What's going to take the pressure off is getting to this dinner, and figuring out whether this guy they've hired really is some hot-shit TEDx-er, with his "Brand Positioning as Predation" videos, or if Elspeth just got distracted by his hair and jawline and shoulders, y'know?

TIM. I remember when I was a genius – with hair and a jawline and shoulders. I don't recall Elspeth getting all flustered over me.

JEN. You're adorable when you're jealous.

> *(She closes the laptop.)*

TIM. I'm not jealous. I just take issue with my exclusion from the sexy genius club.

JEN. You know how Elspeth is. It's primitive. The guy looks like an alpha.

TIM. Colour me reassured.

> *(She hands him his shoes.)*

JEN. Please. Alphas are useless now. What the hell good is the ability to kill a bison when you can order your groceries delivered on the internet? These days the real alphas are identified by their sexy, subterranean pallor. That's the mark of an Internet God.

TIM. I dunno, I think if I were a god I'd be entitled to more handmaidens or something.

JEN. Don't push your luck, buster.

> (**JEN** *starts dragging him toward the door.*)

TIM. Some of them might even be virgins.

JEN. Come on, let's go get a look at the enemy.

TIM. *(As he's pulled along after her.)* Poor guy. He has no idea what he's in for.

Scene Two

(The offices of Belle Vie *– hip, but starting to look shabby in places.* **JEN** *in her office, unhappily staring at budgets.* **BRUCE** *– early thirties, slick-as-hell – knocks.)*

JEN. And you're early.

BRUCE. After the – awkwardness at dinner, I thought we could get some coffee and talk.

JEN. Awkwardness? My publishing board foists you on me without so much as a "By-the-by, Jenny" and you think a quick chat is going to make us best friends?

BRUCE. No. But I like a challenge.

*(***JEN*** doesn't dignify that with a response.)*

A little light reading?

JEN. I'm trying to pull 50k out of our overhead. It's like trying to decide which finger to cut off.

BRUCE. 50k is a Band-Aid on a bullet hole. Your operating deficit is twice that.

JEN. I know how big my deficit is.

BRUCE. No, you don't.

(He pulls a set of papers from his case.)

You scored a couple of big gifts back in 2014, and your accountants have been using them as a buffer, but as of this fiscal your safety net is gone.

JEN. *(Flipping through the papers.)* That's not – Finance would have said something if that were –

BRUCE. Your former GM? She was shopping for her new position for at least a year. My guess? She thought the 100k hole might take the sheen off her CV.

JEN. Oh my god.

BRUCE. Now, I know that comes as a shock, but you don't have to let it knock you back –

(But **JEN** *is already moving on.)*

JEN. Yeah-yeah-yeah. Look. I appreciate the heads-up. And you seem – competent, but you aren't going to charm me into forgetting you're here because the trophy-wife running my board thinks she'd be better at my job than I am.

BRUCE. So, it's not me, it's the rebranding?

JEN. Oh no. It's also you.

BRUCE. You *just* said I was charming.

JEN. Yes. But you're also the kind of patriarchal throwback who uses anecdotes about his hunting trips to justify *laissez-faire* capitalism –

BRUCE. That's hardly –

JEN. You're here to rebrand my magazine and I'd bet my eye teeth you'd never seen an issue before last night –

BRUCE. Hey –

JEN. And I'm pretty sure you're sleeping with the aforementioned Board Chair.

    (A beat.)

BRUCE. …Well.

JEN. These things happen.

BRUCE. Just the once.

JEN. I see. That makes it all alright then.

BRUCE. You didn't like my hunting anecdotes?

JEN. They made you very relatable, if you like that nascent serial killer sort of thing.

BRUCE. You should have stayed for the duck fat ice cream.

JEN. My husband had work to finish up at home.

BRUCE. Your husband? The one with the jacket over the ironic t-shirt?

JEN. He works in games. It's a different dress code.

BRUCE. Married long?

JEN. Five years.

BRUCE. Kids?

JEN. Nope.

BRUCE. Want 'em?

JEN. Big on boundaries, I see.

BRUCE. Happy?

JEN. Ridiculously.

> *(With a huff:)*

Let's get this over with. Go on, roll out Elspeth's plan to turn us into a luxury lifestyle magazine.

BRUCE. Yeah. I don't think you should do that.

> *(A beat.)*

JEN. That's a plot twist. Alright. Impress me. What would Davy Crockett do?

BRUCE. Strip it right down to its core.

JEN. *Belle Vie*'s mandate is "your guide to the ideal life." We don't really go in for austerity.

BRUCE. Depends on whose ideal life we're talking about. Right now, your magazine is all post-modern veneer. It's ironic, clever, and deeply unsatisfying.

JEN. Did you just call my magazine shallow?

BRUCE. Out of touch would be more accurate.

JEN. This from a man whose hobbies date to the Palaeolithic.

BRUCE. The primitive is always compelling.

JEN. So is the aspirational.

> *(Beat.)*

From the time you're a child, what do you imagine except your ideal life? The things you'll do, the people you'll meet, the brave new person you'll be – it's always there, on the horizon.

BRUCE. You think people's ideal lives have anything to do with "The new political avant-garde" or "How to live your life as art" anymore? You might as well be hawking luxury goods. That kind of optimism evaporated in 2008.

JEN. We adjusted our hopes and dreams for the downturn?

BRUCE. Not just the downturn. The environment. The corporate state. Genocides.

JEN. So you think the world is ending and I should rebrand my magazine to match? Oooo. We could call it *The Sandwichboard.*

BRUCE. What I think, is that you are deeply unhappy.

(*Beat.*)

JEN. I'm not.

BRUCE. Everything about you screams it. And it isn't just job stress or your marriage. It goes so much deeper. How long has it been since you felt like that ideal life of yours was in reach? That somehow, despite the climate melting down, real estate skyrocketing, job security vanishing like a pipe dream – there was a way for you to get there? And you aren't alone. There's a whole generation out there wondering what happened to their lives. You need to stop selling them a dead dream, and offer them something they need instead.

JEN. And what's that?

BRUCE. A way to get through it all.

JEN. You want me to start planning the "off-grid" issue?

BRUCE. Maybe. Why not?

JEN. We're a culture mag. Your idea of a good time may be killing an elk with your teeth, but our readers want lit reviews and the hottest new place to have brunch.

BRUCE. Is that what you're looking for?

JEN. That's – not the point.

BRUCE. Your declining readership argues otherwise. I think you are your readers, and I think you know your whole life – the indie rock concerts, the organic produce, the hipster hubby – is on borrowed time. Your prosperity is hollowing out beneath you. And I think you want what everybody wants – a life on the other side.

JEN. And you're going to lead us through the wilderness?

BRUCE. Laugh all you want, but the hunting trips and survival training? What they mean is: I don't need any of this. I don't need people to hire me, or to buy my magazine. I don't need grocery stores or access to an ATM or running water. I don't have to depend on anyone. And when you know that, in your bones? The rest of the noise of life fades into nothing. Leaves you free to pursue exactly what you want.

JEN. And what do you want?

BRUCE. Well, I'm not interested in sleeping with your board chair again.

>   *(Beat.)*

JEN. Still married.

BRUCE. Never said you weren't.

>   *(He gathers up his papers and heads for the door, holding it open for her to come with.)*

Now, are we going to get some coffee and save this place?

>   *(Reluctantly, JEN follows him out.)*

Scene Three

(The loft. **TIM** *coding on the couch, drinking something violently orange from a mason jar.* **JEN** *enters, still unsettled by her conversation with* **BRUCE.***)*

TIM. Hey, sweets.

JEN. Hey.

TIM. Abby called while you were at work.

JEN. Uh-huh.

TIM. I don't think she's coping with the move back to her mom's. She sounded – unstable. Like *Streetcar Named Desire* unstable.

JEN. Uh-huh.

TIM. Okay. What happened?

JEN. *(Distracted.)* What?

TIM. Did round one with Mr. Hair and Shoulders really go that badly?

JEN. Well, the patriarchal cliché figured out our deficit is twice what I thought, so...

> *(* **TIM** *takes a sip of his orange drink and makes a face.* **JEN** *notices.)*

What is that and why are you drinking it?

TIM. Ah. I was looking at this month's credit card bill –

> *(He gestures toward a small stack of bills on the coffee table.)*

– and that didn't seem like the sort of thing I could face without a cocktail. Considering the state of said credit card bill, though, I thought I should try to make do with existing stock.

JEN. Which was?

TIM. Tang crystals and a fifth of gin. I'm calling it the Tang-mosa.

JEN. *(Picking up the bills and beginning to sift through them.)* Resourceful. Sad and desperate, but resourceful.

TIM. Oh no, no, you do not want to look at those.

> (**JEN**'s *eye catches on a figure.*)

JEN. Goddammit. I thought we were cutting back.

> (*She flops on the couch and* **TIM** *hands her the Tang-mosa without a word.*)

This is not where I'm supposed to be right now, y'know? You go to school and pay your dues and work hard. You're not supposed to end up about to lose your apartment, and having some Cro-Magnon question your ability to engage with reality.

TIM. What did he say?

JEN. He said...stuff.

TIM. How dare he.

JEN. It's hard to make a counterargument with a 100k deficit. It's like a scarlet letter, the scarlet "I" of insolvency, or incompetence, or irrelevance –

TIM. So, did Mr. Sexy Genius have any actual thoughts on how to dig you out?

JEN. Yeah. He's got – a plan.

> (*She lets herself sink into his shoulder. Beat.*)

Tim, do you think we would survive...y'know...an emergency?

TIM. What?

JEN. I guess I never thought about it before. But you can't just drift through life expecting that nothing bad is ever going to happen, right? Things happen – like –

> (*She glances around, searching for – or possibly avoiding – something.*)

– like oil spills, and recessions, and earthquakes.

TIM. Yeah. But the government... Ugh. I can't even complete that sentence.

> (*Beat.*)

I guess we're supposed to have a kit? And shoes by the bed for some reason...

JEN. *(Wincing as she takes a sip.)* We can't be that bad. There must be a lot of things we could survive, easy. We'll just start with the simple stuff and work our way up. So...the power goes off! We could totally survive the power going off for a few days.

TIM. Yeah. Yeah... Well...

JEN. Well? Why is there a "well"?

TIM. How much water do we actually have in the apartment?

JEN. Why would we need to worry about water? It's not like the taps would just...

>   *(Off* **TIM***'s look:)*

The taps would stop running?

>   *(Beat.)*

Okay. Okay. So...

>   *(She runs to check the fridge, the sink, the bathroom.)*

We've got the water in the toilet and the gin you didn't use to make the Tang-mosa.

TIM. *(Raising the orange jar.)* Which is truly soul-destroying. I apologize.

JEN. You don't die of dehydration for like three days. We could last for three days.

TIM. On gin and toilet water? I'm pretty sure the gin would make our dehydration worse, and you're not supposed to drink the water in your toilet because of – oh, I don't know, dysentery?

JEN. Fine then. I'll head down to the corner store and buy some bottled water.

TIM. Okay. Sure, but...

JEN. But?

TIM. Do you have any actual cash on you? Or just your credit cards?

>   *(Beat.)*

JEN. Shit.

TIM. Also, we have no flashlight, candles, first-aid kit, or food.

JEN. Hey! I saw some goat cheese in the fridge...but I think it's moldy.

TIM. The goat cheese?

JEN. The fridge.

> *(Beat.)*

Oh my god. If the power went out we'd die up here with our credit cards and dysentery.

> (**TIM** *throws an arm around her to comfort her.*)

TIM. Shhh. Have some Tang-mosa.

JEN. We suck.

TIM. At least we suck together.

> (**JEN** *takes a deep gulp of the Tang-mosa and shudders.*)

How about we put on some terrible movie where Bruce Willis has to save the world from a volcano, and have some epic, the-world-is-ending-and-we're-totally-doomed sex. That could be pretty hot.

> (**TIM** *flips open his laptop and starts searching for a movie to set the mood.* **JEN** *is silent, brooding into the drink.*)

Armageddon? Oh – except Bruce Willis dies – that's always kinda depressing. Also, Ben Affleck. Hurk.

> (**JEN** *doesn't respond. She looks at the credit card bill again.*)

Deep Impact? Euh. Yeah. Morgan Freeman and Elijah Wood. Not so much with the sexy.

> (*Nothing.* **JEN** *puts down the credit card bill and starts to drift around their apartment, considering and then discarding books, records, decor...*)

Day After Tomorrow. The dialogue. *2012*. The plot. *Waterworld*. Euh. The jet skis.

> *(And now* **JEN** *is staring at* **TIM** *as he continues his search.)*

What? You wanna go full-on retro? *Omega Man*?

> *(Beat.)*

Come on baby. The world is going down in flames and all I wanna do is get blitzed and kiss you, isn't that romantic?

JEN. No.

TIM. Hey, I know that wasn't my best pitch, but –

JEN. No, I mean – yes that's romantic, but No. I haven't been working my ass off since I was fourteen to lose my job. Or end up as some shivering loser in a real-life disaster movie.

TIM. Okay. So...what do you wanna do?

JEN. We are not failures. I have never failed a single goddamn thing in my life. Not my driver's license, not a single test in school, not freaking share time in the second grade. Screw "prosperity hollowing out underneath us." This is us. We are young. Successful. Cool. We're going to make this survival bullshit our bitch.

> *(She grabs a pot from under the stove and heads into the bathroom. We hear the sound of a tap being turned on.)*

TIM. Couldn't we just watch *Armageddon* instead?

Scene Four

> *(The loft. An emergency kit stacked into the corner, and the ottoman replaced by two flats of bottled water.* **ABBY**, *fragile and lovely, drinks white wine and watches* **JEN** *stuff emergency supplies into Tupperware.)*

ABBY. Wow. So you're really getting into the prepping stuff, huh?

> *(She looks around for a place to sit.)*

Hey. Where'd that cute little ottoman go?

JEN. Craigslist. It was that or die of dehydration.

ABBY. *(So that's weird.)* Yeah. And anyway, we're all far too attached to material things.

JEN. Abs.

ABBY. I just mean – I never realized how much Raleigh bought for me until I was leaving it all.

> *(Beat.)*

But then you discover you don't need – any of it. That the furniture and the jewelry and the clothes – they are not essential to your being.

JEN. He didn't let you keep your clothes? God, I cannot believe Raleigh turned out to be such a ratfink –

ABBY. Oh no. I could have kept all of it. He even offered to keep paying for the apartment until I was on my feet. But I just – the thought of taking charity from him –

> **(ABBY** *tries to take a centering breath, but –)*

JEN. Charity? Screw that. You should have hired a lawyer and rolled him for half his net worth. He kicks you to the curb and buys a 600k condo for some twenty-two-year-old? If Tim did that to me? I'd pay someone to give him syphilis.

ABBY. Tim would never do that to you.

JEN. Damn Skippy. *(Sotto voce.)* So that's twenty kilograms of rice to use by 2018…

ABBY. Jen – Do you even cook?

JEN. No. But I figure I can start by 2018.

ABBY. It was a different kind of thing with Rawls. Not like you and Tim. You guys are…better balanced.

JEN. You know what you're going to do?

ABBY. That's what I wanted to talk to you about. You remember back in school? Before I, y'know, didn't finish –

JEN. That's the one I could murder Raleigh for.

ABBY. No. I wanted to go travelling with him –

JEN. Bullshit. He liked having you there to coddle him. Hell, I'm surprised he found time for an affair without you scheduling it.

ABBY. But before that. When you were going to be a novelist and I was going to be a child psychologist? And you did it. Kind of. Meanwhile I can't even remember how to want something that much. But there's this course – out on one of the islands – all about finding your path through inner stillness. The thing is, it's like 1500, which is pretty much all I've got.

> *(Beat.)*

Who knew enlightenment was going to be so expensive, huh?

JEN. God, Abby. No. *No*. You are not paying some guy with a homemade hookah your last 1500 dollars to tell you to "follow your bliss." If you want to waste money, pay someone to kneecap the twenty-two-year-old.

ABBY. Jen!

> *(She takes another centering breath.* **JEN** *rolls her eyes.)*

No. I'm not giving in to destructive thinking. I'm practicing gratitude. I am grateful I didn't end up Raleigh's trophy wife.

JEN. Point. Boo to trophy-wifedom. I am going to miss those brunches at the Hawksworth, though. The sablefish benny?

ABBY. Don't remind me. I tried to make one at home – but all Mom had was canned tuna. I ended up crying into the hollandaise.

JEN. The food security thing is depressing. Two people, in a year, need 317 kilograms of carbs. We don't have the cupboard space. Seriously, twenty kilos of flour and sugar alone –

ABBY. I thought you were off gluten. And processed sugar.

JEN. Yeah. But stuff without preservatives keeps for shit. The apocalypse will not be gluten free.

ABBY. And what does Tim think of all this?

JEN. Tim's too busy trying to score a job designing "a little of the old ultraviolence" to get into it.

ABBY. Oh god. Between that and work you must be so stressed.

> *(Beat.)*

We could do the inner stillness course together!

JEN. Screw inner stillness, I'm thinking about urban survival training. There's a school in Seattle where you do a mock evacuation from the city.

ABBY. I never know if I'm supposed to take you seriously.

JEN. Hey. You read the news. We are one good earthquake away from losing everything west of the ninety-nine. And like doing crystal meditation to avoid thinking about how Raleigh left you all helpless and hopeless is any better –

> *(**JEN** catches herself.)*

Oh god, Abs \ I didn't mean –

ABBY. No, you're right. I should take survival training. I'm barely surviving North Van.

JEN. There are ways to fix that, y'know.

ABBY. Yeah – I don't know if I'm ready to evacuate Seattle.

JEN. I was talking about dating. God, the one good thing about the whole Raleigh debacle is I can finally get some vicarious romantic thrills.

ABBY. I'm not sure I'm up for – anything, really.

JEN. Uh. But it would be such a terrific distraction. Right now the only excitement in my life is trying to deflate the ego of this guy at work.

ABBY. The consultant, right? The one who started you in on all this stuff?

JEN. If he weren't practically a Hemingway protagonist he'd be perfect. Raleigh thinks he's got you beat? Let him choke on a hot Eco-anarchist.

ABBY. Jen. It's a breakup. Nobody wins. It's the end of the world.

JEN. *(Triumphantly applying a label.)* Trust me. You can win the end of the world.

> *(Off* **ABBY***'s silence:)*

Everybody competes, Abs. You know as well as I do that the whole "get enlightened" thing is just another arena. Can't get ahead with power or money? That's fine, tell yourself you're a better person.

ABBY. Now I know you aren't serious. Self-improvement isn't some ploy –

JEN. Fine then. No reason to worry you'll be competing with Rawls by flirting with the hot locavore.

> *(***ABBY*** takes another centering breath. Midway through, she catches* **JEN***'s expression:)*

ABBY. I'm not sure you'll like it if I do.

JEN. Wait, what?

ABBY. Remember that guy in second year? Kyle-what's-his-face? Who you spent all of first semester wanting to strangle, but then when he asked me to that art show at the Bau Xi –

JEN. Oh, no. No. This is not that.

ABBY. Jens.

JEN. It isn't!

> *(Beat.)*

Look. Just because I overreacted *one* time –

(**JEN** *might say more, but they're interrupted by* **TIM** *entering, dressed for an interview.*)

JEN. Hey! You're back early. How did it go?

TIM. Well, the good news is, you're not going to have to put up with me making plans for a post-apocalyptic deathtrap in our living room.

JEN. You didn't get it.

TIM. I really didn't.

ABBY. Aww, Tim. That sucks.

TIM. They took one look at my portfolio and said my code was "interesting," but that they were looking for someone with more "bleeding-edge sensibilities."

JEN. Bleeding-edge? Seriously? For a game where a man dismembers animated corpses with a cleaver?

TIM. I guess I was worried too much about the horror, and didn't get the cartoon physics on the decapitations and vivisections.

JEN. Bullshit! You know what it freaking is? You've got too much empathy. These psychopaths are just pandering to some xenophobic desire we've got to shoot other people in the name of survival –

ABBY. Yeah. You don't want to be putting energy like that out into the world.

TIM. It would have been nice to be putting the energy of a 60k contract into the world. Some of us still have student loans.

JEN. Well, you've got too much integrity for that.

TIM. I'm glad someone thinks so.

(*Beat. He looks between them.*)

Aaaand I'm spoiling girls' night, aren't I?

ABBY. Not even a little bit. You can join. We're figuring out how to do green tea facials with just, y'know, green tea.

TIM. Tempting as that is, I think maybe I should hide in the bedroom and play *Civilization* until I feel like I'm in control of my life again.

(He shuffles off. **JEN** *and* **ABBY** *watch him go.)*

ABBY. Poor Tim. He's trying so hard.

JEN. God, yes. It's painful to watch. He's going to be up there oppressing the virtual masses until he finds something else to fixate on.

ABBY. We could put a pin in girls' night – take him out to cheer him up.

JEN. You sure? We'll end up bowling. Or at the Legion, bidding ironically in the meat raffle.

ABBY. It'll be fun. You guys can remind me there's still hope for love in the world.

> *(From somewhere above come the sounds of a video game starting up.)*

JEN. Yeah. A romance for the ages.

> *(***ABBY*** watches as* **JEN** *goes to fetch* **TIM***.)*

Scene Five

(Jen's desk at Belle Vie. **BRUCE** *and* **JEN** *before a whiteboard, brainstorming. Across the top of the board is scrawled "What is the New Ideal Life?"* **BRUCE** *is up at the board writing "Survival" on one side.)*

BRUCE. I didn't think you'd cave so fast.

JEN. It's a disaster kit. It doesn't mean I want to sleep with you.

BRUCE. How about water?

JEN. Three days' worth. Though where you're supposed to keep it all in a 650-square-foot apartment – we don't even have storage.

BRUCE. Not something I have to worry about. I'm a survivalist, not a Prepper.

(He tosses her the dry-erase marker.)

JEN. Because there's so much separation in *that* Venn diagram.

BRUCE. You don't have to stockpile what you know how to find.

JEN. Bully for you, you didn't have to give up your favourite ottoman.

(On the opposite side of the board, **JEN** *writes "Comfort.")*

BRUCE. So you think you're all set now, because you bought a $120 emergency kit, and traded in a footrest for a couple of boxes of bottled water?

JEN. Yes. Because I'm preparing for an emergency, not Ragnarok.

*(***JEN*** *tosses the dry-erase marker back.)*

BRUCE. It's not about that. It's about the probability you're going to need certain skills and resources.

(On the board, **BRUCE** *writes "Security" and tosses the marker back to* **JEN.**)

JEN. There it is. What's the probability the world is going to end? And even if you believe it will, why read us? Why not just get a subscription to *Crazy Bunker People Monthly*?

BRUCE. Because this isn't just about surviving, it's about doing it well.

JEN. So we'll be *Town & Country* for the scorched wasteland?

(On the board, she writes "Culture" and tosses the marker back.)

BRUCE. Crisis is opportunity, and that makes for exciting content.

JEN. Oh my god. You're looking forward to it. You know they shoot the guys with nice suits first, right?

BRUCE. What? I'm not –

(Then, with a shrug:)

Fine. I can admit to a certain amount of – anticipation. When sixty-two people can hoard the same amount of wealth as the bottom three-point-five-billion, it might be time for a little upheaval. I can build a cabin with nothing but a sharp rock. Let the guys who don't clean their own toilets find out what a stock portfolio is worth in a revolution.

(He writes "Agency" on his side and tosses back the marker.)

JEN. So some rich asshat's reversal of fortune is enough to get hyped about the end of civilization?

(Over on his side of the board she writes "Misery.")

BRUCE. What's so great about civilization? You're defending a "culture" that pays some ape on the UFC circuit more than your annual budget to beat other apes with his fists.

*(**BRUCE** snags the marker back and on her side of the board writes "Hypocrisy.")*

JEN. Yeah. Well, the only people looking forward to the post-apocalypse are testosterone junkies who get a little too excited about Ayn Rand.

BRUCE. Sweet talker.

JEN. The only thing I'm *less* interested in publishing than ads for $2000 handbags, is articles valourizing survival of the douchiest.

> *(She snags back the marker and writes "Brutish & Short" in his column.)*

BRUCE. There was some point where survival of the fittest stopped applying? It just shifted from biggest club to biggest trust fund. You want to tell me you don't wake up, every morning, feeling mired in that?

> *(He snags back the marker and writes "Quiet Desperation" in her column.)*

JEN. Am I thrilled about late corporate feudalism? Eww. No. But if the bulk of the species is too selfish and/or willfully stupid to do something about it, I'm not going to waste my creative life trying to change their minds.

BRUCE. That why you don't write anymore?

> *(Beat.)*

JEN. What did you do, pull my bio from 2009?

> *(Beat.)*

I stopped because I spent four years writing a short story collection that netted me six grand. There are easier ways to make almost no money.

BRUCE. I liked the one about the girl driving to the city in the stolen car. The way you talked about the wide open night, and everything possible in it.

JEN. I was twenty-two.

BRUCE. It was more than that. It was the way she wanted to meet the world. Without illusions. Without platitudes. Fearless.

> *(A moment.)*

JEN. Yeah. Well. That book is like a time capsule from when I believed in the meritocracy.

BRUCE. The meritocracy? Really?

JEN. I know. But that was what they sold us. If you were smart, and worked hard enough, you'd get to do what you loved for enough money that you could buy a condo, go on the occasional vacation, and never have to envy anybody.

BRUCE. Ah, the dashed dreams of Generation Xerox.

JEN. Low blow.

BRUCE. Not my fault if your ambitions are predictable.

JEN. And yours aren't?

BRUCE. Self-sufficiency is the only ambition worth having.

(He writes "Self-Sufficiency" up on the board.)

You want a vision of the ideal life that'll sell copy? It starts right there.

(Beat.)

You could come north with me for a weekend, let me show you.

JEN. Yeah? And how exactly should I explain that little business trip to my husband?

BRUCE. He could come too, but that might get awkward.

JEN. You want to convince me we can sell the simple life to urban sophisticates? Come over for dinner. We can do one of those foraging things you keep bragging about. Impress the group, we'll consider it proof of concept.

BRUCE. Because you, me, and your husband at dinner magically gets less awkward.

JEN. I'd set you up.

BRUCE. I can find my own date.

JEN. Eew. No. You're not bringing some sexual drive-by to my apartment. I'll get my friend Abby.

BRUCE. What's wrong with her?

JEN. There's nothing wrong with her.

BRUCE. You're not using her as a beard because she's Eligible Bachelorette number three.

JEN. I don't need a beard. Abby's great. She's just...post-breakup and filling the gaping crater of her dead future with incense and sun salutations.

BRUCE. So...damaged and flailing around for a new identity? Sounds fun.

JEN. Whatever. You're the one who wanted a chance to show off your skills to the untermensch.

> (**JEN** *circles "Self-Sufficiency" and starts wiping down the rest of the whiteboard.*)

BRUCE. I think you've accused me of liking both Ayn Rand and Nietzsche in the last ten minutes.

JEN. If the jackboot fits...

BRUCE. You know you're giving me a hard time because you find my manly competence irresistible.

JEN. Oh. Completely. Take me now, you primitive god.

> (*At the board,* **JEN** *writes "Belle Vie" and then draws an arrow to a new name: "Sur Vivre."* **BRUCE** *gives the new name an appreciative whistle.* **JEN** *tosses the eraser at him.*)

Scene Six

(The loft. Crammed with supplies. **JEN** *and* **TIM** *get ready for the dinner party.* **JEN** *is in the kitchen.* **TIM** *sneaks a bite of casserole before heading back to his laptop.)*

JEN. Booyah. A completely local menu of burdock salad, roast potatoes, and wild mushroom casserole. That'll show him.

TIM. I still can't believe you managed to scrape that together from the park.

JEN. And the Endowment Lands. And stole from that community garden on Homer. Which we tell no one.

TIM. Clearly.

JEN. You think it's enough?

TIM. It borders on food porn.

(Beat.)

It's a pretty sweet spread for a guy you despise.

JEN. It's not about that. It's about making him eat his whole "better-prepped-than-Thou" schtick.

(There's a buzz from her phone.)

He's here. Get the door. I need to change.

(She tosses her phone to **TIM**.*)*

Try not to be too twitchy. It'll ruin the illusion of our domestic bliss.

TIM. Always a confidence booster.

(He swings open the door and looks up at **BRUCE**. *His manhood is totally threatened.)*

Hey.

BRUCE. Hey.

JEN. *(Offstage.)* I'll be right down!

TIM. Smells good. What is it?

BRUCE. Roast duck on a bed of asparagus.

TIM. That's local?

BRUCE. If you've got a garden and a hunting license.

TIM. Which, clearly you have.

BRUCE. What did you guys do?

TIM. Salad. Potatoes. Mushroom casserole.

> *(Beat.)*

Jen doesn't really do half-measures.

> *(There's a moment of awkward guy foot shuffling.)*

BRUCE. So how's the job hunt going?

TIM. The what?

BRUCE. Sorry. I thought Jen said you were job hunting.

TIM. Well, I'm a game designer, and I'm shopping around for my next project. Building my portfolio. Taking meetings.

BRUCE. Guess it just sounded like job hunting to me.

TIM. Yeah. Well. It's going great. I'm considering a few projects. Or, y'know, thinking about maybe designing one of my own –

> *(**JEN** heads back down from the loft, made-up to her very coolest.)*

JEN. Tim's brilliant. So he's careful about the work he picks.

TIM. Uh...yeah.

BRUCE. Good for you.

JEN. Oh my god, is that a duck? Did you kill a duck?

BRUCE. Yeah. You said you liked it.

JEN. ...It's alright.

BRUCE. You said the only reason ducks were on the planet was so they could go in your mouth.

JEN. Well, maybe I'm thinking of becoming a vegetarian. Like Abby, who I'm sure will be relieved that there are some non-duck options on the menu.

BRUCE. I heard. Not bad for your first time out.

JEN. Not bad for any time. Those mushrooms are morels.

> (**BRUCE** *flags that, but* **JEN** *presses on.*)

That is some goddamn gourmet foraging.

BRUCE. I'm just saying that not everyone is ready to make a survival commitment like getting their hunting license and learning to shoot.

JEN. We did just fine without resorting to gunplay, thank you very much.

TIM. You know I was like a *Duck Hunt* wunderkind on the NES.

> (**JEN**'s *phone goes off again.*)

JEN. Oh thank god, that's Abby.

TIM. Still got it up there if you want to go toe to toe.

JEN. Sweetie. Let's not.

> (**JEN** *opens the door to let* **ABBY** *in.* **ABBY** *enters warily, holding a pie plate.*)

Hey. What did you bring?

ABBY. Uh – it's a rhubarb crisp.

> (*Beat.*)

That I cheated and bought at Whole Foods.

TIM. First time out for everyone.

> (*Off* **JEN**'s *cough:*)

Though Jen did make a gourmet casserole.

> (*And* **BRUCE**'s *look:*)

And Bruce murdered a duck.

ABBY. Wow. That's – Duck, huh? Wow.

> (*She extends her hand.*)

Abby.

BRUCE. (*He takes it.*) Bruce.

ABBY. It's funny, I always thought the kind of people who worried about "the end of the world" were, well – nutcases.

> (*Beat.*)

You definitely do not look like a nutcase.

TIM. *(Sotto voce.)* Give him a few minutes.

JEN. *(Wedging herself between* **BRUCE** *and* **ABBY**.*)* Let's get the food on the table, shall we?

> *(During the following the group manoeuvres around the table to finish setting and laying out the food.* **TIM** *pours wine while* **BRUCE** *and* **JEN** *strategically place their dishes.)*

ABBY. So Tim, how's the job hunt going?

TIM. Fine. Just fine.

BRUCE. Tim's picking and choosing.

ABBY. Oh. Because I thought –

TIM. Well, it's not like I'm being that \ choosy.

JEN. We can keep the duck off to the side. After all, Abby can't eat any –

ABBY. It's okay. Bruce probably went to a lot of trouble –

TIM. It's just a difficult time in the industry, \ y'know –

JEN. Please, you've been a vegetarian since first year –

BRUCE. Jen, if the poor girl wants a little duck –

TIM. And you have to be careful what you sign on to –

JEN. The "poor girl" isn't abandoning her deeply held principles –

ABBY. Well, they aren't \ deeply –

JEN. And moral convictions –

BRUCE. No one is asking her \ to –

JEN. Just because you think it's impressive to shoot a three pound bird!

ABBY. *(To cut off the bickering:)* So. Bruce. Jen's pretty excited about this prepping thing – but I never heard how you got started?

BRUCE. Oh – uh – When I was eight, I got lost in the woods. Up near Birkenhead. I almost died.

> *(Everyone swivels toward* **BRUCE**.*)*

JEN. What?

BRUCE. I was that kid, the one you'd see in the news, who'd wandered off from the campsite. RCMP officers with dogs looking for me. At first I wasn't even scared. It was an adventure, like being the star of my own Hardy Boys novel. Then sun went down, and the hypothermia set in. There was this moment – I'd huddled up near the base of a tree, but I was still so cold – and I remember looking up at that huge dark sky through the branches and knowing that I was going to die, and there was nothing I could do about it. When the dogs found me my temperature was barely above thirty. A few more hours, and that would have been it.

> *(Beat.)*

ABBY. Wow, that must have been just –

BRUCE. Yeah.

> *(Beat.)*

That was the moment I realized the world doesn't forgive incompetence. You need the skills to take care of your own.

TIM. I'm sorry – to take care of your own? Look, clearly your childhood was – traumatic. But dude, people found you. You think it's going to be any different after an earthquake or a flood?

BRUCE. Depends on the earthquake. Depends on just how bad things were before it hit. Sure, maybe order reasserts itself in seventy-two hours. What are you going to do if it doesn't? If people start to get desperate?

TIM. Uh –? Help them?

BRUCE. So, just trust in the kindness of possibly armed strangers?

TIM. Possibly armed –? What do you think is going to happen? Seventy-two hours and then society collapses? Are there looters? Is it anarchy?

BRUCE. You think those things don't happen?

TIM. You think they're going to happen here?

BRUCE. I think the possibility exists. And I think Jen agrees with me.

ABBY. You know what I think –

TIM. Jen bought an emergency kit, that is not the same as deciding civilization is doomed, and getting ready for Mad Max time.

JEN. Jen can speak for herself, and you can leave her out of the penis measuring –

BRUCE. It's a good thing at least one of you is taking responsibility –

TIM. Oh, so because I don't have a gun fetish I'm a failure as a man –?

BRUCE. Hunting doesn't make make me a psychopath. Hand someone a .308 and most will be able to tell the difference between you and Bambi –

TIM. Could we not talk about shooting me, maybe –?

BRUCE. Every major conflict or disaster on record the people who have died, died because they weren't capable of fending for themselves. What's your plan?

TIM. Well, it doesn't involve shooting anyone.

> *(Beat.)*

ABBY. *(Has been practicing her breathing as hostilities have escalated.)* You know what? This all looks wonderful. The salad – and the roast potatoes – you know they sell potatoes just like these at that community garden up the way –

JEN. Oh?

ABBY. And the casserole smells amazing.

JEN. Yes.

> (**JEN** *pops up to start ladling the casserole out.)*

Full mouths. Good idea. A little wine, a little casserole. Everybody will feel better –

BRUCE. Yeah. We can't eat that.

JEN. What?

BRUCE. Sorry, I was looking for a good time to say something. Those are poisonous.

TIM. Oh. Sure. Because any food you didn't shoot is immediately suspect.

JEN. No-no-no-no-no. It's all fine. I had pictures. I checked.

(She heads up into the kitchen.)

BRUCE. It's really easy to mistake morels –

JEN. *(Bringing back a bowl.)* For false morels. Like I wasn't going to do my research. See? Perfectly safe.

BRUCE. Okay, you see this fluff on the inside of the stalks?

JEN. But they – I – Oh my god.

BRUCE. Everybody has a learning curve with this stuff.

JEN. Oh my god.

ABBY. At least we caught it before anybody ate any.

TIM. Uh…

(They all turn to **TIM**.*)*

So, how much of that would a guy have had to sneak before dinner to make this a go get your stomach pumped kind of evening?

ABBY. Oh no, Tim.

JEN. Oh my god. I poisoned you? I poisoned him?

TIM. Sweetie, I'm sure it's fine. I ate a few bad mushrooms. I'll be all nauseous and vomit-y and then –

BRUCE. Your liver will fail.

TIM. Holy crap. You poisoned me.

JEN. I didn't mean to!

(Beat.)

The emergency room. We have to go. I just have to –

(She's darting around, picking things up and putting them down in a panic.)

BRUCE. It's okay. I can drive him –

JEN. No! You're guests and – the food is all out – and we were supposed to –

TIM. As the guy with the failing liver, I'd definitely like someone to drive me.

JEN. Yes – I'm so sorry – We have to go. We have to go now.

ABBY. It's okay, sweetie. Go. Take care of Tim. I'll handle everything here.

(**JEN** *grabs her keys and starts leading* **TIM** *out of the apartment. Just as they reach the door:*)

ABBY. Well, I suppose if the casserole is out, I've got no choice but to try the duck...

Scene Seven

(The loft. **JEN** *cleans up.* **TIM** *lies on the couch in a blanket, nursing a cup of tea.)*

TIM. You know, given the poisoning, that went pretty well.

JEN. Sure.

TIM. ...And you were right, Bruce is a halfway cool guy.

JEN. Oh really. So you're not threatened by him now?

TIM. Look, I'm not saying I want to be best bros, but a guy saves you from organ damage, and – you kinda warm up to him. Plus, it's gotta be intimidating to find yourself on a blind date with Abby.

JEN. Please. You cannot seriously think Abby is out of Bruce's league. If anything, it's the other way around. I love her, but Abby's a train wreck.

TIM. Yeah, the kind of train wreck guys fling themselves under.

JEN. Sure. Fine.

TIM. Hey, wait...are you sulking?

JEN. *(Totally sulking.)* ...No.

TIM. You are. You're totally sulking because you lost your little bakeoff.

JEN. Easy for you to say. You weren't the one who made a Near Death Casserole –

TIM. It was an honest mistake.

JEN. Still...

TIM. Well, if you don't want to give it up, I could just start calling you Lucretia.

JEN. You wouldn't.

TIM. Jonestown.

JEN. Ah!

TIM. Wicked Queen.

JEN. Yeah? Laugh it up, Dopey. Just wait 'til you see what I put in your sandwich.

TIM. *(Hand to his heart.)* You're going to make me a sandwich? The man-fairy told me this day might come.

JEN. The man-fairy? Does that mean you're gonna jump in on the survival project?

TIM. Better than that. I had an idea about the job situation.

JEN. Really?

TIM. Yeah. Instead of applying for more of these horseshit franchise jobs, I'm going to start a new project of my own.

JEN. Oh. Well. That's –

TIM. Great. I know. I'm going to build something to give us a leg up with your whole prepping thing.

JEN. *(Unthrilled but trying.)* Oh really?

TIM. Like a survival simulation. Of disasters and our responses to them. And as we develop more skills and store more supplies, we can see how our chances change...

> *(He grabs his laptop and notebook from off the coffee table, wincing with the effort.)*

So first I split up things that could happen into two categories: Fast, like wars and natural disasters, and slow, like escalating fuel and food costs –

JEN. Okay. Yeah –

TIM. The system will obviously be more complex, but – I'll assign timing variables to events – and those values interact – like, here, if I decrease the oil supply, the food costs go way up, and when that hits like a fifty-percent threshold with respect to incomes it triggers food riots –

JEN. So you're planning a really depressing version of Sim City.

TIM. Kind of. With us in it.

JEN. Wow.

TIM. ...And you hate it.

JEN. No – I don't hate it – I – I love that you're taking initiative – I do. It's just – Designing an indie game doesn't solve the whole you having no income thing...

TIM. I know. I know. But I've gotta do something. I can't just lay around here dodging EI calls and building portfolios for jobs I don't even want.

JEN. Well – if you're feeling that way about design jobs, you could always see if you could get something in testing. Or if they'd take you back at Hardware Revolution?

TIM. Hardware Revolution? Are you seriously suggesting I roll back in there with my tail between my legs and beg to go back to upselling laptops to kids with rich parents?

JEN. It's better than lying around moping because the job you want doesn't exist.

TIM. Moping? I'm not moping. You poisoned me!

JEN. Are you serious? As if you've done *anything* but mope for the last six months. Oh, no one appreciates my genius. Oh, no one understands my intellectual deconstruction of communication. Oh, I drank the last beer in the fridge and I'd have to put on pants to buy more –

TIM. *(Struggling to his feet.)* Hey! Like it's a cakewalk with you judging me all the time –

JEN. I do not.

TIM. Every time you have to pay for something because I'm broke you get this pinched, squinty little look on your face, like someone's dog just left a turd on the carpet.

JEN. I do not!

TIM. You do. Especially when it's some expensive thing you want but you know you'll have to pay for it all yourself.

   (Mimicking her:)

"Brunch at the Hawksworth! Mimosas and bennies!" And then the bill comes.

   (He mimes her making a pinched face.)

JEN. The Hawksworth? Try your half of the rent. Try the minimum payments on the cards we've maxxed out – You think I'm rebranding my magazine for the fun of it? Of course I'm frustrated! My options are give up having anything nice because you're broke, or suck it up and pay for you! Why the hell else would I be pissed off about yet another project that'll leave you nowhere near getting a goddamned job!

(There's a beat. Each one of them daring the other to say something worse.)

TIM. I'm going for a walk.

(He heads for the door and then turns around.)

After I put some pants on.

Scene Eight

(The loft. A few days later. **ABBY** *and* **JEN** *with a steaming quart pot and darkly spattered jam-making paraphernalia.)*

ABBY. And he's still up there?

JEN. Sulking. Or building his new "project." Or both. Because the fact that we're presenting the whole *Sur Vivre* concept to my board tomorrow isn't *quite* enough stress.

ABBY. That's the new title? It's clever.

JEN. It better be. It needs to convince them this new mag is going to tap the whole "post-millennial zeitgeist." As though half of them could recognize it.

ABBY. Oh, Jen.

JEN. It's fine. Bruce's concept – *the* concept – is good. So – I'm dealing. We're making jam. Jam is soothing, right?

ABBY. Yeah. And Tim'll come around. He has to. You guys are so good together.

JEN. You really think that?

ABBY. You don't?

JEN. Oh – well – yeah. Yeah.

> *(Beat.)*

It's just – you remember the guys I dated in school, right?

ABBY. Would you say "dated"? I mean, instead of "hooked up with"?

JEN. Thanks.

ABBY. Well...they were very...muscular. And they had a certain –

JEN. They were self-absorbed assholes. Good-looking, self-absorbed assholes. And when I started dating Tim I was all: Look how different he is. Look how he isn't arrogant, and doesn't treat dating like some perverse power game. Like, I've grown up and I'm making healthy choices, right?

ABBY. Exactly.

JEN. Yeah – and it's good. Tim is sweet. And creative. And kind.

ABBY. Tim is all kinds of awesome.

JEN. Except sometimes I start feeling like I just...got scared and gave up on the things I really wanted in a guy –

ABBY. On self-absorbed assholes?

JEN. On guys with some *oomph*. Who don't care if you make a bitchy face because they aren't so goddamn sensitive. Who don't need you to take care of them. Who don't *need* you at all – because they're hot and confident and they can score other girls, but they *want* you.

ABBY. Okay, that last part really doesn't sound healthy.

JEN. God. Who wants to be healthy all the time? No one wants kale and tofu. They want red velvet cake, and lobster, and too many twenty-dollar martinis.

ABBY. Remember how unhappy those guys used to make you? Half the time I don't think you even liked them – you just wanted to prove you could bag them.

JEN. Well...that wasn't the *only* reason.

ABBY. You're just on edge. Tim is sweet, and he adores you.

>   *(Beat.)*

And if he takes to the prepping thing, maybe he'll macho up some.

JEN. You've stumbled onto my diabolical plan.

>   *(They're interrupted by some serious splattering noises coming from the quart pot.)*

ABBY. Should it be doing that?

JEN. I think so.

>   *(They dart over to the pot.)*

Was it supposed to drop that much? We put like a gallon of blackberries in there.

ABBY. I guess some of the liquid – evaporates? How do we know if it's done?

JEN. *(Pulling a chilled plate from her freezer.)* It's supposed to gel on a chilled plate.

> *(She holds it out for* **ABBY** *to drip some jam onto it. The jam doesn't drip.* **ABBY** *shakes the spoon harder. And harder. Nothing.)*

Yeah. So that's probably done.

ABBY. Probably.

JEN. Okay. So now it goes into the sterile jars.

> *(They keep chatting as they spoon the goo into the jars* **JEN** *has prepared:)*

So... While we're talking about testosterone overdose, I thought I'd apologize for the "set-up with Bruce" fiasco.

ABBY. It wasn't really that bad.

JEN. You mean the part where I set you up with a survivalist nutjob? Or the part where I almost poisoned us all?

ABBY. No, I know he isn't going down in history as the most tactful guy ever, but he's also, kinda...

JEN. ...Arrogant? Condescending? Smug?

ABBY. ...Interesting.

> *(***JEN** *freezes mid-jar-filling.)*

JEN. Oh my god. You like him.

ABBY. What?

JEN. You do. He's all good-looking and condescending and you're all hot yoga train wreck and you like him!

ABBY. Jen. You're the one who set me up with him. Wasn't liking him kind of the point?

JEN. No.

> *(Off* **ABBY***'s look:)*

By which I mean *yes*. But just as practice. A confidence booster. You weren't supposed to *like* him like him.

ABBY. Why not?

JEN. Did you miss the survivalist nutjob portion of the discussion?

ABBY. Yeah, but don't you kind of agree with him about that?

JEN. He's a ruthless murderer of helpless animals.

ABBY. One duck! You were eating the leftovers when I got here!

JEN. Just because it's delicious doesn't mean it's alright!

> *(Beat.)*

What I mean is – you're just getting back on your feet. A week ago you were going to give your last dime to some fraud with a man bun. Now you're going to latch on to the first good-looking alpha who drags his knuckles by?

ABBY. Jens. I met the guy once.

> (**JEN** *visibly deflates in relief.*)

JEN. Good.

> *(Beat.)*

Good. Because it's just – you start planning for the end and you have to start thinking – if you wind up trapped in a 300-square-foot fallout shelter, is this really the guy you want to see every day? Grow old with? It's all well and good when it's terrific sex and New Pornographers concerts, but are you going to be happy with him when you're arguing over the last of the freeze-dried kale and how he doesn't have the balls to skin the rabbit? We've got what? Thirty, thirty-five more years until we're decrepit? Do you wanna risk wasting that time on someone it turns out you can't stand?

ABBY. Well, that's bleak.

JEN. That's reality.

ABBY. Maybe it is, but it's also fear talking. And I'd rather be grateful.

> (**ABBY** *looks around and lights on the mostly-filled jam jars.*)

Like: you and I made jam today. No scurvy for us in the fallout shelter.

JEN. *(Looking over the jars.)* Yeah, I think we're not done yet.

ABBY. Really?

JEN. I think we have to put the lids on and boil them again.

ABBY. Everything in those jars has been boiled at least once. Including the jars.

JEN. I know. Ugh! I have no idea how this is supposed to help me survive anything. I need more crap to make it than I ever needed before. And how the hell you'd do it without a working stove is just –

(Beat.)

Screw it. Let's make some blackberry vodka and be grateful for Northwest Cosmos.

ABBY. Yes please. You can complain about Tim, and your big, stress-y meeting, and I can keep thinking of reasons I'll be better off without tall, dark, and ignoring my texts.

(A beat. JEN looks at ABBY.)

JEN. *(Heading for the liquor cabinet and pulling out a bottle.)* When you put it that way, I am definitely going to need a drink.

Scene Nine

(The Belle Vie *offices.* **BRUCE** *working.* **JEN** *enters with a travel mug, spectacularly hungover.)*

BRUCE. You're late.

JEN. So it would seem.

BRUCE. You realize we have less than three hours before we're pitching the new magazine to your board?

> *(***JEN*** responds with a groan as she drops to her desk.)*

What the hell happened to you?

JEN. Abby and I made jam.

BRUCE. In a nightclub?

JEN. I couldn't stare down all that double boiling without fortification. So we got blitzed, like the brave pioneer women used to do.

BRUCE. The night before the biggest presentation of your career. Good choice.

JEN. *(Lethal sarcasm.)* Oh really? The biggest presentation of my career? And I forgot?

BRUCE. Very professional.

JEN. Devastating, coming from the manwhore who slept his way into the job.

> *(Beat.* **BRUCE** *swallows down a retort, then:)*

BRUCE. Drink your coffee and get yourself under control. I have not spent the last two weeks figuring out how to save your ass to have you blow this meeting by acting like a wasted teenager.

JEN. Yeah, well, nobody asked you to ride in here, with your self-reliance schtick, and mess everything up –

BRUCE. Your board did, because you'd let this whole magazine burn before you'd admit you have no idea how to save it.

JEN. Just because I won't sell out everything I believe in a desperate attempt to scrape together operating funds –

BRUCE. Because there's so much dignity in self-sabotage? Christ, this is why sane people shouldn't work in the arts –

JEN. Eew. How the hell did I ever get the idea to set you up with Abby?

> *(Beat.)*

BRUCE. Is that what this is about? Feeling insecure your hot friend doesn't hate me as much as you'd like?

JEN. Please. I'm so the alpha girl. I'm smarter, I'm sexier, \ and –

BRUCE. I know.

JEN. What?

BRUCE. I know. Abby isn't who I want.

> *(So that hangs between them for a moment.)*

JEN. I have a husband.

BRUCE. If that's what you want to call him.

JEN. What else would I call him?

BRUCE. It's ridiculous, you with him. With his cave full of games and self-deprecating humor to cover the fact he's a failure. And you know it.

JEN. Okay. That's not funny anymore.

BRUCE. It's really not. Because you're smart, and sexy. But you're not an alpha. You like that I want you, but you'll never do anything about it. You're too scared to give up your settled little life – or maybe you just don't want to look at your pathetic husband's face when he figures out he was never going to be enough for you.

JEN. Or I just don't find all this retrograde macho posturing as attractive as you think.

BRUCE. Oh. So this is about my failure to live up to some groundbreaking future model for romance? I gotta tell you, Jenny, your whole lock down a husband, buy a condo, go to brunch plan isn't blowing my mind. You talk big, but I can see the duplex and two-point-five kids from a mile away. Because you don't have the balls to come after what you really want –

JEN. God. You are such a complete asshole!

> *(She lunges forward to kiss him. This escalates into behaviour that is not workplace-appropriate, but* **JEN** *balks.)*

No. No. I can't –

BRUCE. Yes you can.

JEN. This isn't – what is this supposed to be?

> *(A beat.* **BRUCE** *can't answer her.)*

Yeah. That's what I thought.

BRUCE. Just because I can't promise you some guaranteed outcome –

JEN. I cannot deal with this right now.

> *(She turns to bolt.)*

BRUCE. And the presentation?

JEN. It's fine. We'll – we'll get through it –

> *(**BRUCE** takes a step toward her and she flinches back.)*

I'll just – I'll prep somewhere else.

> *(She bolts. In frustration,* **BRUCE** *rips the paper he's been working on in half. Then, after a moment thinking about it, he takes his phone from his pocket and begins to text.)*

Scene Ten

*(The loft. Dark. The blue glow of electronics leaching in from the upstairs. **JEN** enters, still carrying her bags from work. She's been out a long time. **TIM** emerges from upstairs.)*

TIM. *(After a moment.)* Hey.

JEN. Hey.

TIM. You're late. Did the board meeting not go –

JEN. I don't want to talk about that.

TIM. ...Okay.

JEN. Look, I know \ you're having a rough –

TIM. I don't \ want to –

> *(Beat.)*

Sorry.

JEN. Yeah.

TIM. I get it. Building the game with these versions of "us," I've been thinking and – I get it. You have this plan. This vision for a life you're going to have – and then it turns out that there's just so much less of everything than you thought. Less good food, less time to travel, fewer chances to make something you can really love. And they all cost you so much more than you ever thought. And I'm supposed to help you: When the food riots hit, I'm supposed to loot the convenience store. When we flee to the mountains, I'm supposed to build you a cabin. When the zombies come, I'm supposed to defend you with a chainsaw. And I want to do all those things. I want to help you the way you help me. Because I don't have a vision of the future without you in it. And I wanna be the guy. The guy you can rely on, the guy you married. And I know I've fucked it up thus far, but I will do anything I can. Loot convenience stores, eat squirrels – you ask and I will do it for you.

> *(There's a pause. **JEN** is silent.)*

TIM. ....Jen? Sweetie?

JEN. ...I think I want a baby.

> *(There's a beat as* **TIM** *gapes in utter slack-jawed horror.)*
>
> *(Blackout.)*

End Act One

ACT TWO

Scene One

(Right where we left off. **TIM** *still gaping.)*

TIM. What?

JEN. A baby.

TIM. What?

JEN. I think I want to have a baby.

TIM. I'm sorry. I seem to be having some trouble with having lost my grip on reality.

JEN. I know it's kind of sudden.

TIM. Really?

JEN. It's just – the more I keep thinking about what things might be like: If everything just keeps getting shittier, and we end up out in the wilderness with no ambulances – and I'm almost thirty and I really, really want access to, y'know, an epidural and a surgeon who knows how to perform a C-section in case something goes horribly wrong –

TIM. Jesus Christ, Jen –

JEN. And I know when we talked about this I wasn't sure I wanted a kid but that was when we were going to go to concerts and eat brunch forever. If it's just going to be this – if it's just going to be struggle and failure and growing old and dying right here, then I need something else. I need something to hope for. I think maybe a baby would be something to hope for.

> *(She's on the verge of breaking down.* **TIM** *rushes down to comfort her.)*

TIM. Oh god. Sweetie. I know. But I'm not sure that "rescue us from the relentless despair of existence" is a good reason to have a kid, y'know?

JEN. So no. You're saying no –

TIM. No. It's not no. It's just – where is this coming from? Did something happen in your board meeting?

JEN. Why does this have to be coming from somewhere? Why can't it just be something –

TIM. It just seems like you're upset – and maybe making huge, life-changing decisions when –

JEN. God! Tim. It was a – a bad meeting. Okay? But this isn't about fixing something else. So if you don't want to do this –

TIM. No. Jen – I meant what I said. About being the guy that you can rely on. About being your husband. So if you think that we should have a baby, if you think that's the best plan...then I'm in. Whenever I think about kids I always think about you and –

JEN. You think about kids?

TIM. Yeah. Sometimes –

> (**JEN** *kisses him.* **TIM** *tries to pick her up. He has trouble with her bags, but manages to get them to the couch.)*
>
> (*Dropping awkwardly onto his back:*)

Ah!

JEN. You okay?

TIM. (*Powering though.*) Yeah. Yeah. Just my – uh – back. I'm good. This is good. Are you good?

JEN. (*Peeling off her shirt.*) Yeah. You picking me up – that was – hot – totally hot – primal –

TIM. (*In an increasing amount of pain.*) Oh yeah. That's me. Primal. Grrrr.

JEN. Probably more primal if we don't talk about it.

TIM. Yeah. Yeah. Of course.

> (*There's hair-pulling and elbows in the wrong places and finally* **JEN** *just bowls* **TIM**

> *over which kinda hurts his back again but*
> *he's going along with it until* **JEN** *heads for*
> *his pants and –)*

JEN. ...Are you not into this?

TIM. No. No, I am. I totally am. You know it just sometimes... S'okay. We'll just do you.

> *(He starts working on the buttons of her*
> *jeans.)*

JEN. ...Okay...yeah – or no.

TIM. No?

JEN. Well, given the project it kinda defeats the purpose.

> *(She swats his hand away, stuffs her hand*
> *into his pants, and starts working on the*
> *problem.)*

Come on, baby –

TIM. *(Wincing a little.)* Okay, maybe we could ease up on the "baby" talk, given –

JEN. Wait, so that's a turn-off –?

TIM. No. Not a turn-off. Just pressure I don't need. C'mon. Let's do you. That always gets me going –

JEN. *(Pushing* **TIM** *away.)* No! I already said I didn't want that if you weren't –

TIM. Okay. Really? Like when has that ever been a problem before?

JEN. Yeah, because on top of everything else I'm so selfish?

TIM. That is not what I'm saying! I didn't say that!

JEN. That is exactly what you're saying –

> *(She shoves him away, which clearly aggravates*
> *his back.)*

TIM. Auggh!

> *(**JEN** is mutinously silent. **TIM** slumps and*
> *winces as he pulls at his injured back.)*
>
> *(The silence is interrupted by a beep from*
> **TIM***'s phone. He checks it.)*

TIM. Oh. Well that's perfect.

(Off **JEN***'s look:)*

Simulated you and me just starved to death in our fallout shelter.

Scene Two

(A little table at a bar. **BRUCE** *and* **ABBY** *with cocktails.* **ABBY** *fiddles with her drink.)*

ABBY. Oh god. That sounds terrible.

BRUCE. Yeah, nothing like bickering during a presentation to really sell a concept.

ABBY. It's not like Jen to lose her head.

BRUCE. It was a – stressful situation.

ABBY. And you still don't know what the board is going to do?

BRUCE. Nope.

ABBY. I can't believe you're so calm. I would be having a panic attack. A huge, ongoing panic attack.

BRUCE. You get used to it. Besides, you can always find some way to distract yourself.

ABBY. I see. So I'm a distraction?

BRUCE. Is that the kind of man you think I am?

ABBY. It's possible I've been warned.

BRUCE. What? Jen told you I'm some predatory womanizer, out to break hearts?

ABBY. Jen didn't say that.

BRUCE. Yes she did.

ABBY. Yes she did.

> *(Beat.)*

She's looking out for me. I'm not exactly in fighting form these days.

BRUCE. Is that what you want? Someone to look out for you?

ABBY. I don't know. I used to think so.

BRUCE. How are you and Jen friends? You're very – different.

ABBY. Well, we met in university and she was just always so smart, and so driven. I never had that. And yeah, she can be judgemental – but she was the only one of all my friends who told me not to leave school. Everybody else was all: Seize the day. Grab the rich guy. Like they knew it was the best chance I'd ever get. Jen thought I could do better. She expects everyone to do better. I think the world is very disappointing for her sometimes.

BRUCE. I think she has a talent for making it that way.

ABBY. That's not fair.

BRUCE. You don't think she'd hate that you're here with me?

ABBY. She'd be worried I was making the same mistake I made with Raleigh.

BRUCE. And what mistake was that?

ABBY. Avoiding responsibility for my own life.

BRUCE. That's not something I encourage.

ABBY. No, I guess you wouldn't.

>   *(Beat.)*

What's it like, dating in the end times?

BRUCE. Dating hasn't changed. It's always been survival of the fittest.

ABBY. Not very romantic.

BRUCE. Neither is dating.

>   *(Beat.)*

When people "fall in love" it's just because they've found a collection of traits that are acceptable based on their own social capital. Whether that's a strong set of shoulders or a diverse stock portfolio, the calculations are very similar. For instance, you might like me because my jaw and shoulder ratios indicate I produce a lot of testosterone.

ABBY. Oh really? That's why I like you?

BRUCE. It marks me as a successful organism. And everybody wants as much as they can get out of a potential mate.

ABBY. People aren't like that – at least some people aren't – they fall in love and stay together. Like Jen and Tim.

BRUCE. The ones who do that just think there's greater survival value in stability.

ABBY. Wow. You really think that.

BRUCE. I think it's infinitely preferable to know exactly what you value in another person and what they value in you. To pretend that love is unconditional is at best a delusion, and at worst a snow job.

>   *(Beat.)*

ABBY. Alright. So what exactly would you value about me?

BRUCE. You really think you want to hear that?

ABBY. I spent the last five years with a man who treated me like I was precious and fragile. Which was all well and good until that included lying to me and cutting me loose with no life skills at all. Maybe brutal honesty is exactly what I need.

BRUCE. Brutal honesty?

ABBY. Just seems healthier.

BRUCE. I like that you're genuine, that you don't hide that you're struggling. I like that you're very beautiful, but you haven't fished for a compliment all night. I like – that you're interested in a challenge.

>   *(Beat.)*

ABBY. So if I agree to a second date, am I going to have to hike for miles and wrestle a cougar?

BRUCE. You think you'd be up for it?

ABBY. I'd like to be.

BRUCE. Whether Jen approves or no.

ABBY. Jen's tough. She'll get used to it.

Scene Three

(The loft. Several days later. In addition to the food and water stockpiles, there's camping and survival gear, which **JEN** *is cataloging. The blue glow continues upstairs, and a number of cables drip down, running to unknown destinations amidst the supplies.)*

*(***ABBY*** drinks tea while* **JEN** *organizes.)*

JEN. ...And so of course she comes back with a "compromise" that really isn't a compromise at all: I can have "my" rebranding if I increase ad space by fifty percent. I swear to god, she wouldn't care if we were publishing excerpts of *Mein Kampf* as long as we've got a half-page spread for her friend's handbag boutique.

ABBY. What are you going to do?

JEN. Well, If I refuse, they're going to fire me. And if I go along with it I'll have the artistic credibility of a Triscuit. I am aggressively not thinking about it. I am aggressively not thinking about a lot of things.

(Beat.)

ABBY. So. The wires are new.

JEN. Yep.

ABBY. What's Tim using them for?

JEN. He's farmed together a bunch of secondhand servers for the simulation.

ABBY. The video game of you guys in a bunch of different disasters?

JEN. Yep.

ABBY. Is it me or is it kind of warm in here?

JEN. It's not you. They're radiating. Servers radiate.

ABBY. Well – shouldn't we check on him? I mean, how do we even know he's alive in there?

JEN. As if I'm that lucky.

ABBY. Jen!

JEN. Wait for it.

> *(Beeps and buzzes emanate from the loft. The blue glow dims. Several equipment crashes follow.)*

TIM. *(Offstage.)* We're dead!

JEN. What got us this time?

TIM. *(Offstage.)* Meteorite! The fallout shelter needs to be deeper, and we need warmer coats!

JEN. I'll put them on the list!

> *(**JEN** makes notes on a whiteboard list jammed into one corner. Something electronic revvs up in the loft. The blue glow gets brighter again.)*

ABBY. Jen. This is scary.

JEN. And you haven't been trapped with it for the last three days.

> *(Beat.)*

It's better than having him down here, trying to convince me he doesn't find the idea of breeding with me repellent.

> *(Before **ABBY** can object:)*

So! What did you want to talk about?

ABBY. What, me? Oh. Nothing.

JEN. You sounded so happy on the phone.

ABBY. Oh no. It was just, y'know, sunny day. Good kombucha...

JEN. C'mon. I could seriously use some happy –

> *(Beeps. Light dimming. Crashes.)*

TIM. *(Offstage.)* Dead again! Dirty bomb! Iodine and gas masks! This is worse than playing *Oregon Trail*...

> *(Revving. Lights.)*

JEN. *(Adding the items to the chart.)* I swear to god, any of this actually happens, the fallout is not what is going to kill him.

(Beat.)

JEN. Seriously, what the hell could be so bad that you don't want to tell me...

> *(But something in **ABBY**'s expression causes **JEN** to trail off...)*

ABBY. It wasn't like I planned it! \ He called me!

JEN. *(Accusing.)* You're back with Raleigh!

ABBY. No! Not Raleigh!

> *(Beat.)*

JEN. Oh.

ABBY. Jen?

JEN. I just – I thought we'd agreed that it wasn't a good idea. When did this even happen?

ABBY. Last night. We'd been texting.

JEN. Last night. And you –?

ABBY. Went to Opus. I'd almost convinced myself it couldn't be as nice as I remembered.

JEN. *(With a stunted little laugh.)* Terrific.

ABBY. Jen, are you sure you want to talk about –

JEN. Of course I do. I set you up. Vicarious romantic thrills, remember? And after Opus?

ABBY. ...His place.

JEN. Ah. Nice. You realize he booty called you.

ABBY. It's not a booty call if you make plans for the weekend.

> *(Beat. Off **JEN**'s expression:)*

I don't even know if I like him – but I like who I am when he's around. And I really want you to be okay with that.

JEN. Me? Okay? Why wouldn't I be okay?

ABBY. Jen.

JEN. This isn't university. We are not having another Kyle situation.

(Beat.)

But no blaming me when his idea of a date is a night at the gun range.

ABBY. Thanks.

(Beat.)

And, y'know, it isn't all about hot sex with the cute locavore.

JEN. Uh! Rub it in, why don't you?

(Beeps. Light dimming. Crashes.)

TIM. *(Offstage.)* Contagion! More wet-wipes and a decontamination shower!

*(Revving. Lights. **JEN** drops her head into her hands. **ABBY** pats her back and encourages her to take a centering breath. Off **JEN**'s look:)*

ABBY. Oh sweetie. Maybe you and Tim just need a change of scenery? Bruce is going to take me camping up north this weekend. Maybe you guys could come along. Like a double-date? I bet you'll both feel better getting away from all this for awhile.

JEN. Yeah. I'm not sure that's a good idea...

*(**TIM** bursts from the loft entrance. He's in his boxers and clearly hasn't shaved in several days.)*

TIM. I've done it!

JEN. ...Done what?

TIM. Saved us! We live! Ice Age, Volcano, Tsunami, Epidemic, Nuclear Winter – You name it! We make it our bitch, baby!

JEN. ...Yaaay?

TIM. Hell yes, yay! Oh. Hi Abby.

ABBY. Hi Tim.

*(From the loft behind **TIM** comes the familiar chorus of beeps and dimming lights. **TIM** darts back into the loft.)*

TIM. No! That's not happening! It's not! I had everything perfect – it was all –

> (*A series of thumps and crashes. Slowly,* **TIM** *re-emerges. He looks at* **JEN.***)*

You left me.

JEN. I what?

TIM. You took the pump-action shotgun and the grade-A military rations, and you left me.

ABBY. Does he mean in the video game?

JEN. Simulation.

TIM. I can't believe you left me.

JEN. Hey! Abby just invited us to come on a camping trip!

Scene Four

(A clearing. In one corner, **BRUCE** *has constructed a fairly textbook-looking tarp shelter. In the other corner,* **JEN** *and* **TIM** *are constructing a shelter as well – though theirs looks...unstable.)*

JEN. *(Sotto voce.)* Look. Just let me help with –

TIM. *(Sotto voce.)* It's fine. I can handle it –

ABBY. *(To cover.)* This is gorgeous. You totally undersold the gorgeous. This is going to be the prettiest survival training weekend ever.

BRUCE. It's going to be something, alright.

JEN. I cannot believe the way you are overreacting –

TIM. Oh. Is that what's happening here?

ABBY. It'll be fine. A little fresh air, a little sunshine, and they will snap right out of it.

TIM. Oh. Don't let us ruin your trip. I know Jen couldn't stand it if we were a burden.

BRUCE. *(Sotto voce.)* I am not teaching either of them to shoot. Even if it might be an improvement.

ABBY. *(With a smack to his arm.)* Don't be a psycho.

*(**JEN** is watching **BRUCE** and **ABBY**. **TIM** catches her at it and stops holding the sticks she's tying together. Part of their "shelter" collapses.)*

JEN. C'mon.

TIM. So I suppose that's my fault?

JEN. I swear, if you don't stop sulking...

TIM. What are you going to do? Leave me?

JEN. You have been punishing me for days – and now our completely innocent friends, by the way – over something a simulation of me that. You. Created. Did.

(Beat.)

TIM. Thirteen times.

JEN. *(With a noise of incoherent frustration.)* It doesn't matter how many times! You made it up!

> *(Beat.)*

Now, Abs and Bruce have been nice enough to invite us up here, and we are ruining their weekend –

ABBY. Oh, no, I wouldn't say –

BRUCE. I would –

JEN. So I am going for a walk to calm down. And when I get back, we are going to behave like pleasant, friendly, *sane* people. Because if you can't, you won't have to worry about me leaving you, because I'm going to murder you out here in the middle of fucking nowhere and feed you to a goddamn bear!

> *(**JEN** storms off, direction unknown.)*

BRUCE. One of us should probably –

ABBY. I'll go.

> *(Off **BRUCE**'s look:)*

She can't have gone far.

BRUCE. Come back quick if you don't catch up to her.

> *(**ABBY** nods and heads after **JEN**. **TIM** starts fumbling around with the tarp again.)*

Look. You're gonna want to start with support poles.

TIM. I've got it.

BRUCE. By positioning the support poles.

TIM. I have literally designed entire worlds in code. I can turn four pounds of nylon and some sticks into shelter.

> *(While he's speaking, **TIM** jostles the "tent." It collapses.)*

Goddammit, how can I even be this useless? She's right to leave me.

BRUCE. Okay. Man – you do know she hasn't actually left you, right?

> *(As he speaks, **BRUCE** comes over and starts setting the collapsed shelter to rights.)*

TIM. Yeah. Well, she should. I'm pathetic.

BRUCE. You ever think that maybe you'd both be better off?

TIM. Excuse me?

BRUCE. Look at you. How long have you been twisting yourself out of shape for a girl who's only with you because five years ago you looked like her idea of a husband?

> (**JEN** *reappears at the edge of the clearing and hangs back, listening in.*)

TIM. Okay. Now I'd like you to stop talking, because when you say things like that I want to kick your ass, and that would probably end badly for me. Jen's not like that.

BRUCE. You're telling me things weren't great when all she wanted was someone who sounded smart at parties and could score good tickets for the show? But now that the job is getting rocky and real life looms, that she's not thinking about the real estate, the RRSP, and the kid?

TIM. You're an idiot.

BRUCE. I think you mean asshole.

> (*He's got the tarp shelter up.*)

TIM. No. I mean an idiot, who's probably never managed to have anything resembling a long-term relationship. Because all you're describing is how every relationship goes. At first, everything is one big party with this new person. But unless you're some emotionally-stunted man-child who cuts and runs at the first sign of disappointment, that's not the whole story. You get to know people and they get to know you and nobody gets to be exactly who they wanted to be – because you're messy and flawed and on the verge of turning into an old person who will need real estate and an RRSP and – if you get old enough – a kid to take care of you. And if by some stroke of extreme luck, that person you bullshitted into liking you turns out to be someone like Jen? Then you just do your best to keep up. Because, seriously, dude, except for the "hot alpha" thing, this whole log-cabin deer-hunting bit looks a lot like the real estate and the RRSP plan from two hundred years ago. You know, before feminism and television and penicillin.

(**ABBY** *bounces up behind* **JEN**.)

ABBY. Oh thank god. I thought we were going to have to send out a search party.

JEN. Sorry – I wasn't thinking.

ABBY. All good. This place is gorgeous – you can definitely see the appeal of the simple life.

JEN. You ever think that back when things were "simple" we spent a lot more time marrying our cousins and dying in childbed?

TIM. But the menfolk have laboured mightily, and behold: Shelter!

BRUCE. Yeah. Shelter.

(*Beat.*)

So that's our first step for survival. What do we need next?

JEN. Water.

TIM. Food?

ABBY. A nap?

BRUCE. Fire. Fire means warmth, safety, emergency signal. Jen – how about you and Tim dig out a pit. Abby and I'll gather fuel.

JEN. Sure.

ABBY. (*As she and* **BRUCE** *head off into the woods.*) You know, just because I liked the duck, doesn't mean I'm going to let you shoot a deer. You'll be lying in wait, and I'll be hiding nearby, and when the deer shows up I'm going to pop up screaming "Run Bambi's mom! Run!"

BRUCE. Okay, you do know that we're not hunting deer, right? At most, we're going to shoot a groundhog, or a rabbit –

ABBY. Oh! Thumper!

>*(**TIM** starts clearing a pit for the fire. **JEN** comes over to help.)*

JEN. Hey.

TIM. Hey.

JEN. Thanks for sticking up for me back there.

TIM. Yeah, well. Husband.

>*(Beat.)*

Look, I know I've been acting like an asshat for the last couple of hours –

>*(Off **JEN**'s look:)*

Or days.

>*(Off **JEN**'s new look:)*

Or like a week.

JEN. Maybe I have too. Between the mess at work and the money – and I know in the grand scheme of things it could be so much worse – but I can't stop wanting my life back. And my husband back. That brilliant guy I married, I miss him.

TIM. I know. I just – the thought of you leaving me –

JEN. In a simulation –

TIM. When you build a simulation you build a whole world. You build your best understanding of how the world works – and what does it mean that I can't imagine a world where you stay with me?

JEN. God. That you have low self-esteem, or that you build me up too much? I hear the way you talk about me, like I'm going to save you somehow and – Tim, I am just this girl who's probably about to lose her job and who can't keep carrying you while you build imaginary worlds because –

TIM. Because I can't deal with real life? Is that what you think? I build games because I can't control my real life?

JEN. I just think – maybe sometimes you make worlds that are easier. That demand less of you. Which is fine, except reality isn't like that.

>   *(Beat.)*

TIM. How in the hell did you ever think we could have a kid? If that's what you think of me? How in the hell did you think we could survive anythi–

>   *(TIM freezes.)*

JEN. What?

>   *(Following his eyeline.)*

Is that a rabbit?

>   *(TIM makes a shushing motion. Then, very quietly:)*

TIM. And you're wrong. You hear me, Jennifer Anne Green? You're wrong, and I'm going to prove it to you.

>   *(He sneaks over to Bruce's pack, wrestles out the rifle and loads it.)*

JEN. *(Also whispering.)* Tim! What the hell?

TIM. You think I can't be a provider? I am going to really, actually shoot and skin Thumper!

>   *(Beat.)*

I probably shouldn't have given him a name.

JEN. Tim! This is insane. You don't even know how to use that thing.

TIM. It can't be that different from Call of Duty. It's a point-click interface. Okay. Just point and click. Point and –

>   *(BRUCE re-emerges, carrying an armful of wood. Behind him, ABBY.)*

BRUCE. Jesus Christ! Tim. Put that down.

TIM. No. I'm hunting our dinner.

BRUCE. You don't even know what else is in that direction.

JEN. See. You could kill somebody. Stop it.

ABBY. Tim. No. That rabbit never did anything to you.

TIM. I know. But that doesn't matter when the tribe has to eat.

JEN. We aren't a tribe.

ABBY. There are veggie dogs in Bruce's truck.

BRUCE. You can learn to do this properly, later –

TIM. I have a good shot!

JEN. You have no way of knowing that!

ABBY. No. Tim. You're a sweet guy. You're not the guy who shoots the cute bunny. You're the guy who thinks about his little bunny face, and the broken heart of his little bunny wife.

TIM. Oh. Why'd you say that?

BRUCE. C'mon man, give it up.

> *(Slowly, carefully, **BRUCE** takes the gun from **TIM**. Checks it. A beat.)*

Actually. He's right. This is a pretty good shot.

> *(He takes it. **ABBY** gasps. **TIM** clutches his head, reeling from the sound.)*
>
> *(Blackout.)*

Scene Five

(The same evening. **JEN**, **ABBY**, *and* **BRUCE** *clustered uncomfortably around the fire. In the dark behind them,* **TIM** *works away at something that sounds...squishy.)*

ABBY. You know, Tim... We've got lots of food already. Hot dogs and veggie dogs and s'mores –

> *(Squelch.)*

So there's really no need for you to –

TIM. I'm proving a point.

ABBY. Well, I'm sure whatever it is, you've proven it. Right Jen?

> *(Another squelch.)*

Right Jen?

JEN. Oh. Totally. I have never been more attracted to you than I am in this moment.

TIM. You're not talking me out of this. If Bruce can pull the trigger on a big-eyed, fluffy-tailed –

> *(He retches. Pushes it down.)*

– then I can clean and dress him...

ABBY. But –

JEN. Just let him. He's made up his mind that mutilating an animal corpse will make him a man, and not a character from *Silence of the Lambs*.

BRUCE. It's really not that bad –

JEN. Oh no. You do not get a vote on this. As the psychopath who blew away Thumper, leading us to this heartwarming moment, you don't get to say anything that isn't convincing Tim to lay off the disemboweling!

> *(Behind them,* **TIM** *yelps.)*

Oh god, what now?

TIM. *(Pained.)* Nothing. Nothing. Do we have a first-aid kit?

> *(***JEN*** *drops her head into her hands. She starts to rise.)*

ABBY. You know what. I've got this. Neutral party and all.

*(She heads for **TIM**, who is curled over his hand.)*

Come on, Tim. Let's take you down to the lake and get that washed and patched up.

*(**ABBY** leads **TIM** off.)*

BRUCE. And here I thought you and I would be the awkward part of the doomed romantic weekend.

JEN. I'm actively hoping for the end of the world. It'd put me out of my misery.

*(**BRUCE**, meanwhile, has gone to clean up the mess of the rabbit.)*

BRUCE. You say that, but you couldn't just let it happen. You'd do whatever it takes. It isn't human nature to give up on our own survival.

JEN. Whatever it takes, huh? Is that your way of saying "take the deal, honey"?

(Beat.)

BRUCE. Increasing ad space is better than rolling over and dying.

JEN. Is it? Because I have no idea why I'm doing any of this anymore. Doesn't matter if it's stockpiling canned goods or fighting Elspeth over what we put in a broken-down magazine – or trying to convince myself that Tim is ever going to be more than Tim. Sweet, and funny, and always in need of somebody to take care of him. I am so sick of taking care of him.

BRUCE. You could always stop.

JEN. It's not that simple. You can't just grab a bug-out bag and flee your own life.

BRUCE. Why not?

JEN. Because – the world isn't actually going to end. That's just some escapist fantasy. We've been obsessing about it forever. Before the 2012 thing there was the millennium and Nostradamus... The Romans spent like half their time predicting the fall of Rome.

BRUCE. Rome fell.

JEN. It's because we feel trapped. There's this – mess between us and who we want to be. Crappy boards and spoiled bosses, and behind them crooked governments and huge corporations – and we can't fight them. So we imagine something bigger than we are – fate or nature or god – that'll sweep the slate clean and let us start fresh. What if the only thing worse than an Apocalypse is no Apocalypse? Your life going on and on just the same as it ever did.

BRUCE. So don't wait for it.

>   *(Beat.)*

If this were it, right now: The end of the world, the meteorites arcing down, what would you do?

JEN. If there wasn't going to be a tomorrow?

>   *(Beat.)*

BRUCE. It could be happening right now. Somewhere out there in the dark, a war could be starting, or a vial could be dropping in a bio-bunker, or tectonic plates could be shifting – and maybe all that's going to be left is you, and me, and whatever we decide to make of the world that comes after.

>   *(He's definitely leaning in to kiss her.)*

JEN. Are you seriously making a "last night on earth" pass at me? Like that morbid Romeo and Juliet crap ever works.

BRUCE. Romeo and Juliet were amateurs.

>   *(A moment. **JEN** surges forward to kiss him. **BRUCE** lifts her up and carries her off into the dark.)*

Scene Six

*(The campsite, the morning after. **JEN** sits
by herself in front of the dead fire pit. **BRUCE**
emerges from his tent. He's shirtless.)*

BRUCE. *(Quietly.)* Hey. Where'd you go last night, after –?

JEN. *(Manoeuvring them away from the shelters.)* Abby
and Tim came back while you were hanging up the
food and the goddamn rabbit. I pretended I'd gone to
sleep –

BRUCE. I'm sure you could have come up with some excuse –

> *(He leans in to kiss her.)*

JEN. What are you doing?

BRUCE. Well, given last night –

JEN. Last night was – reckless.

BRUCE. But kind of inevitable.

JEN. Really? Like sleeping with you was some kind of
foregone –

> *(He cuts her off by kissing her.)*

– conclusion.

BRUCE. Isn't it a relief to be with someone who can keep
up? It is for me. And you've got to admit, the sex was –

> *(He's leaning in again. She's almost
> mesmerized. But she shakes herself back to
> alertness.)*

JEN. Ugh. Yes. It was good. You really know how to put
your penis in a woman. But what's going to happen if
your girlfriend and my *husband* find out?

BRUCE. They're both asleep. And they're going to find out
sooner or later.

> *(Beat.)*

JEN. Why would they find out?

BRUCE. Because you're – I mean, you're cutting him loose –

JEN. Oh my god. What do you think is going to happen? That I'm going to drape myself across your manly arms while you laugh and kick sand in Tim's face?

> *(Beat.)*

Ugh. That's why you're so psyched about all this, isn't it? Because you're Moses, right? Leading the rest of us through the desert, showing us your new way to live. And I'm the hot chick with a shotgun to watch your back? Or maybe just lounge around the foot of your throne with Abby, like the bimbos on the front of a goddamn *Conan* novel. God, I'm an idiot.

BRUCE. That is not what I –

> *(Jen and Tim's shelter rustles.* **BRUCE** *turns toward it, but* **JEN** *pushes him away with a –)*

JEN. Don't even think about it.

> *(***TIM*** *emerges with a bandage wrapped around his hand.* **BRUCE** *scoops up a bucket and heads off.* **TIM** *flags* **BRUCE***'s exit.)*

TIM. You guys are up early.

JEN. Yeah.

TIM. Though I guess you crashed pretty early last night –

JEN. I was tired.

TIM. Oh. Yeah. Sorry about the whole "Thumper" mess.

JEN. Yeah.

TIM. Possibly the most traumatizing experience of my entire life, by the way. I feel like writing the directors of every horror movie I've seen to explain that their work did not remotely desensitize me. In fact, I think it's the opposite: I'll be watching movies and video games where people are killing things and all I'll be thinking is "Dear God, do you know how much *work* that would be?"

JEN. The charms of disemboweling are lost to you forever.

TIM. Utterly.

> *(Beat.)*

But if you think this is me giving up, I'm not. Maybe I'm not exactly Survivorman here, but I'm going to get it. Like right now, I'm going to go see if Bruce needs help with –

JEN. No!

TIM. What?

JEN. No. I – You don't have to do that anymore.

TIM. But you said –

JEN. I know. I know I did. But now I want to stop. I just want to go home and lie in our bed and not have to do any of it anymore, okay?

> (**TIM** *gathers her up in his arms to comfort her.*)

TIM. Oh sweetie. Of course. Whatever you want.

JEN. I don't want to not be us anymore.

TIM. We're still us. We're right here. Me with my silly beard and my jokes and you with all the sarcasm and these little flowers in your hair.

> (*He reaches up to touch one and promptly draws his hand back.*)

Or burrs. Definitely burrs. But still, y'know, fetching. Very wild woman of the woods.

> (**JEN** *hides her face in his shoulder.* **ABBY** *emerges from her shelter, yoga mat in tow.*)

ABBY. (*Off the sight of the pair of them.*) Oh! Look at you guys. Seriously. I'm about to die from the adorableness.

> (**ABBY** *lays out her mat and starts into a low-impact yoga routine.*)

TIM. Funny, because I'm about to die watching you be all health guru at the butt-crack of dawn. Am I the only one who'd rather be having huevos high-life in a warm bed?

> (**JEN** *raises her hand.* **ABBY**, *still going through her yoga poses, does too.*)

TIM. Say what you will about the unspoiled beauty of nature, the selection of brunch cocktails sucks.

 (**BRUCE** *returns, water bucket in tow.*)

ABBY. *(Looking at* **BRUCE.***)* Seeing some definite perks to the State of Nature here.

 (*She bounces over to snag a kiss.*)

You're looking a lot more *energetic* this morning.

BRUCE. Sure.

TIM. Huh. Seems like everybody was wiped out last night.

JEN. It was a long day yesterday.

TIM. ...Yeah.

ABBY. Hey! But today we're going to cook up some pioneer-style oatmeal and then bliss out in nature, right?

BRUCE. And I thought we were here to learn actual survival skills.

JEN. I think after yesterday, we've survived enough.

BRUCE. Because survival situations just dissolve when you change your mind about them.

JEN. We're not in a survival situation. The implosion of my professional life does not mean a bear is going to eat me.

BRUCE. Funny, because that's exactly what'd happen to you and Peter Cottontail over there if you were alone out here –

ABBY. Bruce! You don't mean that!

 (*To* **JEN***:)*

He doesn't mean that.

BRUCE. Yeah. No. I don't mean that. I guess I just – I thought the weekend would turn out differently. That's all.

ABBY. I know. But we can still have a good time.

 (*She begins rustling through some clothes in their tent.*)

C'mon, pop on a shirt and we'll go.

> *(She holds one out and then considers it more closely.)*

Oh. Maybe not this one. It's got burrs all over it –

TIM. Burrs.

> *(**TIM** knows. He looks at **JEN**, and maybe if she were in a better place she could fake her way out, but she isn't and she's utterly, utterly busted.)*

> *(**TIM** looks from **JEN** to **BRUCE** and back again and dissolves in a stream of pathetic, hysterical laughter.)*

ABBY. Tim, are you okay?

TIM. No. I'm an idiot.

> *(To **JEN**:)*

That's why you want to pack up and go home, right? Because we're done here. The test is over.

JEN. I didn't mean for any of this –

TIM. Are you insane? You meant for all of this. You pushed at every last step and you knew – you knew there was just \ no way –

ABBY. Okay. What the hell is going on right \ now?

JEN. I wasn't pushing. I – didn't know what I wanted.

TIM. You needed me not to measure up so you'd have an excuse.

JEN. That isn't –

ABBY. An excuse? What are you even talking about?

TIM.	**JEN.**
Burrs.	Nothing!

TIM. My wife fucked your new boyfriend.

BRUCE. Jesus.

JEN. Christ – real mature, Tim.

TIM. Oh. I'm sorry, am I not being cool enough about your adultery?

ABBY. Adultewhat? This is \ insane.

BRUCE. Look, it's not like it was –

JEN & TIM. *(To* **BRUCE**.*)* Shut up.

TIM. Oh Tim, I'm so stressed out by the state of the world. Maybe I just need to make crappy jam and learn to cook house pets and to screw some stereotypically hot guy who's not you to feel okay about it all.

ABBY. I think I'm going to be sick.

TIM. You think you'd be embarrassed to end up such a cliché.

JEN. Fine – You're right. I'm the bad guy. I just… I wanted to feel like the girl I used to be…the one who would never have settled – not that you were even settling at the time…because I loved you and I was happy. I was. Until I wasn't. And this didn't make me happier. It's just – he looked like the life I gave up when I chose you.

> *(**TIM** absorbs that like a shot to the gut.)*

BRUCE. Look, guy, I'm sorry. I know it's harsh but –

> *(**BRUCE** is cut off as **TIM** flings himself at the larger man with a desperate, feral scream.)*
>
> *(They stagger together into Jen and Tim's shelter, which promptly collapses under them. **ABBY** and **JEN** scream.)*

ABBY. No! No! This isn't the way to deal with this – Deep breaths! Deep breaths!

JEN. Tim! Stop it! You're going to hurt yourself!

BRUCE. Dude, listen to her –

> *(This only spurs **TIM** on further, and **BRUCE**, who up to this point has only been holding him off, hits him back. **TIM** reels. **JEN** wades in and slugs **BRUCE** in the gut.)*

JEN. Don't you hit him!

BRUCE. Are you on his side? How are you on his side?

TIM. She is not on my side!

> *(**TIM** flings himself at **BRUCE** and gets popped in the face. **JEN** slugs **BRUCE** again.)*

JEN. I said, don't hit him!

BRUCE. He hit me first!

ABBY. Could everybody please just stop hitting everybody else?

TIM. I do not need your help! I can do this by myself!

JEN. Are you serious?

> (**TIM** *swings for* **BRUCE** *and partially connects, injuring his wounded hand. Reeling,* **BRUCE** *retaliates and accidentally hits* **JEN**.)

Ow! Sonuva –

> (*She kicks him in the shin.*)

BRUCE. Ow! Jen! I didn't mean to –

> (**TIM** *takes advantage of* **BRUCE**'s *distraction and swings again. The three of them topple into the additional shelter, a mass of hitting and biting and "ouching." Desperate,* **JEN** *struggles free and lunges for the water bucket that* **BRUCE** *lugged back, but before she can douse them with it –*)

ABBY. Stop it! This is not how civilized people act! Stop-it-Stop-it-STOP-IT!

> (*For a moment, everyone freezes.*)

Now you listen to me! I don't care what kind of twisted psychodrama you guys are acting out – this has to stop! You came up here because you wanted to be the kind of people who survive the end of the world – and maybe I don't get that, but I know it means you have to be selfless, and cooperate –

> (**TIM** *opens his mouth to object, gesturing from* **JEN** *to* **BRUCE** *and back again.*)

I don't care! I don't care what stupid, slutty thing Jen did because she was feeling insecure. If we're going to be worthy of surviving anything, we have to be better than this!

*(There's a beat. Then **JEN** reaches into the bucket, pulls out a handful of muck and lake weed, and smears it on **ABBY**'s face.)*

*(**ABBY** shrieks and lunges for **JEN**, claws out. **BRUCE** and **TIM** resume trying to strangle each other.)*

(Brief blackout.)

*(Lights up. An unknown amount of time later. **ABBY**, **TIM**, **JEN**, and **BRUCE** sit as far from each other as the destroyed campsite allows.)*

ABBY. I can't believe we're this awful.

TIM. I'm getting there.

ABBY. We're like those people who get trapped by a snowfall and eat each other to survive the winter.

BRUCE. Don't kid yourself. This kind of stupidity took the Donner party months to achieve.

JEN. If it comes to that. Eat me first.

BRUCE. Jen –

JEN. You know, if you could never speak to me again, that'd be great.

TIM. Oh really, so the end of the world has lost its romantic glow for you, has it? No more dreams of an underground bunker built for two?

JEN. Tim –

TIM. You know what I can't believe? I can't believe that all this time, I've been worried about you leaving me.

*(**JEN** watches **TIM** limp away in the falling light.)*

Scene Seven

(The café table. **ABBY** *and* **JEN**, *at brunch at the Hawksworth, with sablefish bennies.* **ABBY** *seems at home.* **JEN** *seems listless.)*

ABBY. ...And so the condo's on the market and we're looking for a new place. I'll have to meet with the realtor after this –

    (Beat.)

Jens? You okay? Too much hollandaise?

JEN. *(With a sigh.)* Can there ever be too much hollandaise?

    (Off **ABBY**'s *look:)*

No, this is wonderful. And really sweet of you given the whole –

ABBY. Please. Who was that guy? Besides. The camping mess was the best thing that could have possibly happened to me. I got home, miserable and disillusioned, and there was Raleigh, sitting on my mother's stoop. He went from creep to Prince Charming so fast my head spun.

    (Beat.)

And I know I'm disappointing you. But we were together for five years – I know what my life looks like with him. And yes, maybe it's not wildly fulfilling, but it's a good life. A comfortable life.

JEN. Guess it's nice that someone got something out of it.

ABBY. Have you talked to Tim yet?

JEN. After the most awkward ride home in history? No.

    (Beat.)

But I have so much work, y'know. Closing down the magazine.

ABBY. I was so sorry to hear about that.

JEN. Yeah. I mean, *I* was done for anyway.

    (Beat.)

JEN. I was headed in that Monday to tell Elspeth that I'd rather watch her run *Belle Vie* into the ground than take that deal. Turned out that between tanking readership and overpriced consultants, we already had.

    (**JEN** *shrugs.*)

I've got offers from some online mags. So, if I really want to, maybe in three years I can be exactly where I was three months ago.

ABBY. Do you know what you want to do?

JEN. About Tim? About any of it? No. This wasn't supposed to be my life. Unemployment and adultery and failure – they were supposed to happen to other people. When did Tim start to look like settling? He was the guy who built worlds for me. My partner for the win.

ABBY. The win?

JEN. Yeah. The win.

ABBY. God. Jens, how do you "win"?

JEN. I don't know. You have a great house, and a husband that everyone wants to fuck, and a pair of cute kids – and a dog, and a job where you help people, and every Sunday you and all your friends go to brunch and you have the sablefish benedict –

ABBY. And you don't have to sell out for any of it –

JEN. Not a bit. And you never grow old, get sick, or die.

ABBY. Of course not.

    (*Beat.*)

JEN. Except lately, I keep wondering, when did my dreams get so small? It's like – when I was little, I'd get up on Saturday mornings and watch these brightly coloured cartoons full of rockstars and explorers and superheroes. And I thought that was going to be my life. This amazing, neon-bright adventure where I got to save the world. I remember it in school, this clear, bright purpose – did I lose it when my stories didn't sell? When I saw how starved that life would be, and found something safer? As if a job could protect me from housing crashes and scarcity and one-percenters? When did I get so scared that I stopped trying to build a better world and started getting ready to live in the aftermath?

ABBY. *(Gesturing to the restaurant.)* As aftermaths go, it could be worse. And maybe that's just growing up. Realizing that you have to do what you can with what you have.

JEN. You never think of your own life as a limited resource.

> *(Beat.)*

I guess you made the smarter play there.

ABBY. I guess I did.

JEN. Trophy wife.

ABBY. Adulterous failure.

JEN. At least there's brunch.

> *(They keep eating in silence.)*

Scene Eight

(The loft. Dark, except for the blue glow coming from the stairs.)

*(**JEN** enters, sets down an empty bag, looks around. She sighs and starts selecting a few choice items to pack up. This is what she's doing when **TIM** enters, dressed as though he's just come from work.)*

TIM. You're here.

JEN. Yeah. Sorry. I was giving notice – Thought I'd pick up some stuff.

(Beat.)

It looked like you were out.

TIM. Working.

JEN. You finally landed one. That – that's good.

TIM. Not really. Hardware Revolution.

(Beat.)

Not my finest hour.

JEN. Oh, well –

TIM. Yeah, after the guys at the Cyborg Werewolf franchise passed, it seemed like the writing was on the wall. So today I convinced a liberal arts major she needed enough RAM to start her own space program.

JEN. It's still good. That you're trying.

(Beat.)

And there's always building an indie.

TIM. Seems like I should learn to cope with this world before I go dreaming another up.

JEN. I guess. What about the –?

TIM. The –?

*(**JEN** gestures in the general direction of the loft.)*

Oh. You mean, have I tried to sell the sprawling life-simulator that essentially chronicles the end of my marriage? Yeah. Not quite there yet.

JEN. Sorry. How are they doing? Digital us?

TIM. They're okay, I guess.

>	*(Beat.)*

I'm fixing up the bunker. You've hiked out to the Cascades. You're getting really good at deer hunting.

JEN. Wow. Yaaay little us, huh?

TIM. Well, they're programmed with every survival skill I could cram into them. I think little you can fly helicopters.

JEN. She's probably got me beat personality-wise, too.

TIM. Hard to tell. She hasn't really interacted with anybody since she left.

JEN. Oh.

TIM. Well, the adultery options out there are mostly mutants and bands of roving cannibals, so...

JEN. Guess I'm lucky the world didn't end.

TIM. Seems so.

>	*(An awkward moment.)*

JEN. Okay. Yeah. Well. I guess this is the stuff I needed – and I should just –

TIM. Yeah.

JEN. Thanks for – making me cool enough to fly a helicopter.

TIM. Yeah.

>	*(**JEN** heads for the door.)*

We're really narcissistic, you know?

>	*(Off* **JEN***'s look:)*

People. We're always saying the world is ending. The world isn't ending any time soon. Just us. Just people. We had this awesome thing and we squeezed everything out of it and now it's ruined. But it's mostly only ruined for us. That's not the world ending. That's just us being jerks. Too stupid to save ourselves.

JEN. Some of us kind of have it coming.

TIM. It's not all bad, though. 'Cause once we're gone, then maybe the world will think of something better.

JEN. Something that would care about more than its own ambitions.

TIM. Something that could face its problems, instead of escaping into fantasy worlds.

JEN. Something that'd be happy with what it had instead of ruining it.

> *(Beat.)*

TIM. Were you really so unhappy? What didn't you have that you wanted?

JEN. Me. I guess. The person I was supposed to be. I just – I want so badly to be the me you see. The one that can walk across the Rockies and hunt deer and fly a goddamn helicopter. Because she wouldn't have cared that her perfect little life was collapsing. She'd have found a way to carry you too.

TIM. She hiked out into a post-apocalyptic desert to get away from me.

JEN. Maybe there were things she needed to learn out there, in the desert.

TIM. Jen.

JEN. Maybe she's coming home. Thinking about how much she misses you when she rolls into her sleeping bag at night –

TIM. Jen.

JEN. Maybe she's standing at the door of your bomb shelter, and she's sorry she didn't do better, that she's not as steady as you – not as good.

TIM. Jen, I –

JEN. It's your bunker. You can let her in or you can shut the door and leave her outside. That's up to you. But she's finally figured it out: Sure, she can survive on her own, but the world might be worth rebuilding with you.

(**TIM** *steps forward, about to close the door.*
JEN *bows her head.*)

(*But he hesitates.* **JEN** *looks up, puzzled.*)

TIM. Maybe he's afraid that if he lets her in, it'll be just like
before. She'll be selfish, and he'll be scared, and they'll
both just wind up disappointing each other.

JEN. Maybe they will. Maybe they're doomed.

(*Beat.*)

Then again, they already survived the end of the world.

(*The light falls on them, there in the doorway.*)

End